MIDNIGHT
AND THE
MACHINE

**A COLLECTION OF SHORT STORIES TO READ
LONG AFTER THE SUN GOES DOWN**

All stories ©2007, except

"Howey's Island" and "The Master Key ©2015

ISBN-13: 978-0979135293
ISBN-10: 097913529X

Published by Studio Szabries

10 9 8 7 6 5 4 3 2 1

Please contact Studio Szabries at
727-895-2444 for special sales, promotions,
appearances and bulk purchases.

They're all for you, Mom
Especially this one.

Love ya,
Yerson

Contents

ALWAYS IN YOUR THOUGHTS

My mind wanders quite a bit. No really, it does and not the way you're thinking. You could even say I'm absent minded and you would be both wrong and right in your assumption. See, my mind wanders into other people's minds. I have no idea how it does, or why it does, but the fact that it does is undeniable. Right now my mind is roosting in a young woman's head. It feels kinda nice to be in her mind. She's young and pretty and all the men do double takes when she walks by. I feel her nicely wide, child bearing hips sway rhythmically with each step and I know that they have yet to deliver a soul into this screwed up world. There's a heaviness between the hips too because she's on her cycle and she fairly pissy about the men ogling her. She feels like a piece of meat and in a way, she's right. She's a meat bag connected to a brainstem and right now, I'm crowding into her cranium having the ultimate voyeuristic experience. She's pretty hot, too. Even though I'd love to run her hands all over her body, and maybe even give her an orgasm, her bad attitude is becoming tiresome, so my mind wanders back into my own head again.

Some time ago, I realized that my mind had made

like Nancy and put on its walking boots. It sounds really cool, but I can tell you, the first few times it was alarming to say the least. I thought I was going crazy. I was certainly going somewhere, but crazy wasn't the place. Where I was going was into other people's heads. No, I wasn't reading their thoughts, I was in.their.head. Move over brain, you have a visitor. Not always a welcome visitor either. Sometimes I'm like a salesman who gets his foot in the door and wont leave until you buy whatever I'm peddling. Or like a mother in law who wont go home until she completely ruins the whole first half of the game. Sometimes the mind I visit welcomes me, grateful for an "original" thought. Either way, the mind I visit pulls up it's knees and grudgingly makes room for me.

How did this happen? No idea. I was just walking down the crowded street one day, heading downtown and bam! The next second I'm swaggering uptown with a rhythm and diddy-bop that this classically white guy has never felt. I looked down at my dark brown hands, felt the big salami in my pants bumping against my leg and I knew something was very amiss. I turned around and saw myself turn around and when I looked into my own eyes from through this guy's eyes, the whole world tilted on its axis and we both nearly fainted. Then it was over. I was staring at the black guy who was pleasantly inviting me to perform some sexual act on myself in exchange for staring at him and everything was back to normal.

Weird.

Yep. I've officially lost it.

But, I didn't really lose anything. I gained something very useful, although it took a cruise into the heads of that old guy, the cute little girl, and the bank manager to realize the potential of this new little trick my mind was playing. There's nothing quite as useful in today's coldly materialistic world as the combination to a bank vault. I'm a pretty quick study and by my fourth foray in the depths of someone else's head, I saw the enormous potential. I read about the bank manager in the paper a few days later. He swore his innocence up and down, and presumably still is from his metal cot bolted to the wall, but the cameras don't lie. And he really did throw the money into the dumpster, like he claims, and someone else got it. If you guessed the lucky trash picker was me, well then you get a prize. Besides, the guy was a pervert. I assure you he will be very happy with his new friends in his new concrete and steel home, even though the food probably sucks.

So you might be sitting there thinking: yeah, all this is very selfishly beneficial to me but what about morals? What about the right thing to do? I can answer with some pride that I have done the right thing. I let that old lady spend her whole monthly check at the track. She didn't win, but hey; that's life. It's not like I could get into the horses head and make him run faster. Or can I? Hmm…I may have to try that someday. Then, I gave that woman the courage she needed to leave her husband who was so annoyingly smarmy. I mean c'mon, who still acts like that, kissing and holding hands after three months of marriage? It was sickening. And, I helped that little boy get rid of his bothersome sister. Now he can play with all the toys. See? I'm a helpful guy.

So today I'm sitting in the college student's head writing this. He's doing the physical writing, but I'm the one whispering the story to his neurons. Who better to tell my tale than some pompous English major? At least the tiresome nerd will get the punctuation right. He might even get a Peabody or whatever the hell award it is they give to the self satisfied authors in their tweed jackets. It will have to be awarded posthumously because when it's done he's going to walk in front of a bus. What? I can't let this guy walk around wearing his writing medal and pontificating on about how the greatest story ever told just popped into his head. Besides, I'm ready to evolve. The split second before he walks in front of the bus, I'm outta here. I want to see if I can be a true free thinker and just float around out there.

Imagine the feeling of exhilaration as I slip these mortal bounds and zip around at the speed of thought. I might drop in on the President of the United States of America or, I dunno maybe the mayor of some little town in Utah or maybe just some regular person. Like you, for example. After all; are you sure you're reading this story or is it reading you?

THE NOTE

I labored over the note for some time. A long time, actually. Probably too long. It was filled with my thoughts and emotions, but it was as empty as a beer bottle in a weed-strewn lot because I would never give it to her. I knew that yet I kept writing and editing and writing it again. Even the pen and paper seemed to know, but the pen was obliged to supply ink and the paper bound to accept it. They had their purpose: record the note. I had mine: write the note.

After the note was finally done, I carefully tore it into tiny pieces and flushed it down the toilet. Before the tank was refilled, I started on the next note.

THE LONG WALK HOME

She balance beamed down the railroad tracks just because she could and because it reminded her of when she was a little girl. Each step put her three feet closer to the love she walked away from two months earlier. It was so much easier back then. Get in his truck and go. A spray of pebbles spun off the back tires and a cloud of exhaust and she was gone. A cheap magician's trick that didn't make the rabbit disappear, but her life as she knew it. Easy to do, not so easy to undo. But sometimes the hard decisions seem easy when you make them.

So now it's one foot in front of the other and stay on the shiny rail. One step closer to home. A gritty walk down a dirty rail line. At least the trees are pretty dressed in their fall best and the birds are singing like there's no reason not to. It would be easier, and more romantic to ride the freight train, like some tired country song, but there hasn't been a train on this line for twenty years.

It seems like there hasn't been a lot of a lot of things around here for twenty years. This town didn't just die, it was beat to death. Faded going out of business signs in grimy downtown storefronts only tells part of the story. The even grimier bars with the faded and dented pickup trucks out front at three in the afternoon tell the other part. Half of this town decomposed long ago and the other half is busy preserving itself in alcohol.

How was she supposed to know? The flowers and the soft words whispered in the dark and the strong arms wrapped around her never gave a hint. The crooked smile and the rough hands so much like her daddy's and the faded jeans filled up just right all made her weak in the knees and blind where it mattered. They say love is blind, but sometimes it's just plain stupid. But she's no dummy. Young and smart she is. So how does a smart girl take off and leave everything for a failed drunk who never grew up or stopped playing cowboys and Indians? The answer doesn't come easy but there are more than enough miles to go to think of one before home slowly appears in the hazy distance.

He was a dream come true, really. Not the cowboy, but the one she left in a cloud of dust. A kind and strong and gentle man, and compassionate. A family man without one, but a burning desire to make his own. A man as sweet as summer rain and true as the flag flying on the Fourth of July. He loved everyone. He even loved the ugly little dog that came to his garage and stayed because he gave it the rest of his homemade lunch one cold October day. But mostly he loved her. He told her she was his twinkling star that fell from the sky and brightened his whole life. Yet, in an instant she snuffed out that light, and sure as if she kicked his little dog, she hurt him to the core. And for what? A fleeting dream that turned to a nightmare.

One foot in front of the other. Three days now

sleeping rough and so hungry. They say fasting clears the mind but hers is muddy like the lazy water drifting past in the brown river on her right. The tracks are long gone, turned north sometime yesterday and now this ugly road next to an even uglier river leads her way. The cars blow past her some with the droning sound of their horns chasing them. The big trucks are worse. The little hurricanes that follow them buffet her and threaten to suck her into their slipstream. The collection of trash on the roadside keeps her mind busy wondering how does someone lose only one shoe and where is the poor kid who belongs to the lonely little broken toy?

Her mind needs to stay busy otherwise it drifts back to the sickening possibility that he won't have her back. And who could blame him? She kicked him in the balls. She kicked his little dog and she kicked his heart right out of his chest. Not physically, but she might as well have. At least that's what she thinks anyway. Not really sure at all because all she did was leave him that stupid note. A coward's way but it was easier and what would she have said to his face anyway? It all amounts to the same thing. There one night enveloped in his glorious arms, his scent making her swoon, and the next in the cramped cab of a pickup that reeked of stale sweat and cigarettes.

The big truck hissed to a stop up the road from her and the passenger door opened with a disembodied arm. The adrenaline squirted into her blood and her heart did the only thing it could and raced up a few beats. This was not a good idea at all. Yea, Last time she got into a truck it turned to crap, but this was different. This guy is a real stranger. Staccato visions of crime scenes decorated with half-nude and dead females capered around in her head. Then she thought: screw it. What's the difference? Dead on the side of the road or dead in the soul it all amounted to the same thing. Besides, if the trucker didn't kill her, it would get her home faster. She jogged to the waiting door and reached for the chrome grab bar.

A tan lined face smiled at her from around a cigarette. What else to do but smile back? She tried to make herself as small as possible in the big cab as the trucker manhandled the rig through its gears. He flicked his smoke out the window and reached into his breast pocket for another. Cupping his hands, that should have been on the wheel, around his smoke he glanced at her sideways and struck a match. The flame met tobacco, its task completed, and out the window it went. In a blue cloud the inevitable questions were delivered on a gravelly voice. Where ya from? Where ya goin? What's a little bitty pretty like you doin out on a night like this? She lied through them with such ease that she almost believed herself.

Wouldn't it be nice if the lies weren't? Back home to the family after a visit with more family somewhere far away. Just a girl with not a lot of money but a big heart going to see sister or auntie or cousins whatever way she could. But there is no family at her back or on her way. Family is what other people have and what she had taken from her long ago. Now, the only hope of growing a new one lies beyond the reach of this big truck's headlights. Hope that lies in a dwindling light fallen from the sky.

Her neck's sore when she wakes up, she's starving, her mouth tastes like the inside of an old shoe and she has to pee. The gentle droning of the diesel engine was gone but not the stink of it. She looked out through the bug guts at the truck stop at thanked God she at least wasn't dead. Or worse. She opened the big door and jumped down and was hit with a blast of exhaust fumes and the rumble of other engines idling around her. She made her way inside looking for her chain-smoking driver but he was nowhere to be found. The bathroom is disgusting and the toilet worse, but it's better than the weeds by the railroad tracks. She hovers through her necessary functions then splashes some water on her face from the stained sink and finger brushes her teeth. She glances in the mirror and then turns to go.

When she opened the door a fat nurse in a stained uniform looks at her with disgust. Shaking her head, the nurse reaches for her and a strong hand grips her elbow. She allows herself to be guided down the hallway back to her little room.

Duncan and the Watch

Duncan found the watch near the soccer field. He didn't play soccer. No, not Duncan. He wasn't really into sports except for the stats. He was more of a brain. Ok… he was an outright nerd. Skinny, glasses, pants too short and gangly all over. But, he was smart. Scary smart. This kid could do huge numbers right in his head without a calculator. And when I say big numbers….I mean BIG. Like a million something times a thousand something equals whatever. He wasn't one of those…um..whaddya call em? Savants...no, not a savant because he was smart at everything, and it seemed, not dumb at anything. Except girls. But maybe he was too young still. I dunno what age they start with girls these days but I figgered by twelve he shoulda been at least noticing them. All in good time, I spose. I said he wasn't into sports, but I meant he didn't play sports. Too skinny. And uncoordinated. But he loved to watch and he loved the stats. Holy cow, this guy could tell you not only how many touchdowns Brett Favre threw, but when he threw them and for how many yards. I'm lucky if I can remember if Green Bay even won last week. But I liked him. Duncan I mean, not Favre. He was a good kid, never in trouble, always said yes please and no thank you. I like that in a kid. It's rare these days.

I never had kids of my own. Always wanted one or two, but my wife packed up and left one day and I never bothered to go out and get another one. They seem to be a lot of trouble and damn expensive to keep around so I just have my cat. He's not too much trouble and pretty much takes care of himself. Once in a while he'll curl up on my lap, usually during the game, but mostly he's off doing whatever it is cats do when nobody is looking.

In fact, it was the cat that got me and Duncan together. Seems the cat was down at Duncan's house mooching food and I guess the kid knew the cat was mine so he brought him back for me. I gave Duncan a buck for his effort, like a reward sorta even though the cat wasn't really lost. Cats are never actually lost anyway. They always know exactly where they are, it just might not be where you want em to be. In any case, it was worth the buck cause now I had at least a little idea what the cat did when I wasn't looking.

Anyways, I tinker with stuff in my garage and that's where I was when Duncan brought Max back. Max is the cat. I named him after that Mel Gibson movie, but Max is never mad. Why should he be? He gets fed for free, gets to go out whenever and has the run of the house. He's got a pretty sweet deal, you ask me. So, I got the garage door up like I do sometimes to let the fresh air in and the cig smoke out. Yea, I smoke. I know it ain't "kool"… ha ha… anymore, but I do anyway. Old habits die hard. I guess old habits can make you die hard too, but that's another story.

I'm in there working on this four wheel contraption that I been wrenchin on for a few years. Its kinda like a car, with four wheels and two seats, but made from bike parts and I been working on a old yard tractor engine for it. That's what's been takin me so long. The engine. I'm tryin to convert it to one of those hydrogen powered setups to save on gas which is through the roof already and no end in sight. Friggin A-rabs really got us by the balls.

So this kid walks up with Max looped over his arm looking all dopey, Max that is, not the kid. Max always looks dopey. and he says

"Hey Mister" (hey mister? Is this kid Beaver Cleaver or what?) Is this your cat"

"Nope" I chuckle "He's his own cat, but yea I suppose he lives here. Where'd ya find him?"

"Down at my house. My mom was feeding him".

"What was she feeding him to?"
The kid tilts his head a bit and just looks at me.
I chuckle again. "Nevermind. Big mistake. Feeding him. He might be your cat now"

"Uh. I can't keep him. My dad doesn't like cats"

I inform him that I was joking and after I wiped my greasy hands on my pants, I took Max off his hands and chucked him in the house. Max, that is. I didn't chuck the kid into the house. Not yet anyway. That was later.

So Duncan takes a long look at my contraption and right away gets down on his haunches and starts muttering,

"The atomization of the hydrogen is causing a vapor barrier that won't allow the proper combustion to occur in time with a mechanical valve assembly. Two possible solutions: increase atomization at the molecular level, which isn't practical because of the primitve conversion

method or substitute hydraulic valves."
I think you can guess that my jaw hit the floor.

    I said, "Huh?"

And he repeated it word for word. I asked how he could possibly know that by just looking and he just shrugged it off and said it was obvious. Obvious?? I've been staring at this little tractor motor for over year and I didn't have a clue. But the more I thought about it, it made sense. I started thinking. Now, this is a slow process for me. I'm gadgety smart, but quick I ain't. Guess you could say I'm no rocket surgeon. I'm more like a big truck going up a hill. I gotta run through the gears starting at the lowest range and then my brain finally picks up speed. This thought though, about the valves, I gotta pull over and park for a second. There are a whole lot more questions I got for this kid first.

I said, "How do you know so much about engines? And how did you even know this thing was hydrogen powered?"

    It's not written anywhere on the engine, and the only way you would know is if you knew about hydrogen and saw the tank and the conversion I did on the carb from plans I found on the net.

He starts looking embarrassed and mutters

"Saw the tank and the carb conversion that looks like it came from hydrogenpower.com"

A whistle escapes my lips. Right on the button. Ok, so at least he's not like psychic or anything. But still, a kid his age knowing about hydrogen conversion? I guess it's possible. My idea was that kids these days just plopped down in front of the game box and deep fried their brains. Hell, this kid could prolly write video games. Maybe he did. For all I knew, he was hacking into the Pentagon in his spare time. We talk for a bit more. The usual stuff,

    "What's your name?"

"Duncan"

"You live down the street?"

"Yessir"

"Your dad drives that GMC, right?"

"Yessir"

"How old are you Duncan"

"12"

I was a bit surprised. I had him pegged for ten, maybe eleven, tops. He was small for his age.

I wink, "You got a special girl at school, Dunc?"

"Uh". His face turns pink. "Um, sir could you please call me Duncan instead?"

"Sure thing Duncan. As long as you stop calling me "Sir""

"Um. Ok Mr. Uh…"

"Name's Charles Hampton. If I had any friends, they'd call me Charlie, which I hate, so you can call me Chuck."

"Uhm…ok. Well I gotta go Mr. Hamp…I mean Chuck"

I chuckle. "Just Chuck….forget the Mister busyness, Ok?"

"Uh…ok, well bye"

"Cya"

So I shift the old brain back into first and start grinding the gears about those valves and pretty much put the kid out of my mind. I got thirsty around third gear so I went inside and grabbed a beer. The beer made me hungry, so I shut the garage door for the night and went inside and fed me and Max. Max scammed some table scraps off me too. I tell ya, he's got the sweet deal here.

About two weeks later and fifty bucks, plus shipping, lighter, I was bolting the head back on the little tractor motor when Duncan came ambling up the driveway.

"Hey Dunc. Sorry. Duncan"

"Hi Mr. uh…Chuck. How's the engine coming?"
I told him that I found some hydraulic valves on ebay and just finished puttin em in. He said that was great and how soon before I could start it up. I told him I had a few more adjustments to do so it wouldn't be tonight. Truth was, I didn't think it would be this month, but why disappoint a kid if you don't hafta?

Duncan looks embarrassed again and says

"Mind if I try?"

Well, I got a lot of time in this thing and yea the kid seemed smart but I didn't want any bolts stripped or anything. I told him I don't think it's a good idea and maybe he should ask his dad first before he gets all greasy. And besides…what if the kid busts a knuckle? Last thing I want is for him to get hurt working on my stupid contraption that will prolly never run anyway. He says his dad doesn't really care what he does. I'm not buying this, but I see my hand extend from my body, like it has a mind of its own, and next thing you know the wrench is changing hands. He gets down on his knees and starts tightening up bolts. He looks around and asks for a torque wrench, which I hand to him, and then a screwdriver and then a ratchet. Before you know it, I go from the inventor to the helper to the tool hander. Hmm…boy's good with his hands, I think as I'm watching this nerdy little kid whiz through stuff that already would have taken me a week. He sure seems to know his way around the tools. So I go inside for a beer and then the phone rings and I figure its Duncan's mom and I should send him home. I don't think she's got my number, but I guess when your kid is somewhere your parent radar kicks on. But it's not her it's some A-rab trying to sell me something. As if they don't take enough of my hard-earned already with the whole oil bit. Can't tell what it is he's peddling cause his English a little off. Why in the heck these people hire phone salesman that cant speak-a da englis, I have no idea. I hang up in the middle of a word that sounds like it could use a few more vowels and head back to the fridge. I reach for the handle but my hand never makes it because just then I hear my little motor turning over. I run out to the garage and just as I'm about to go ballistic on the kid for cranking the motor before it's ready, the thing actually turns over. No kidding. It starts. Four maybe five cranks and the thing is running. And it's not coughing and sputtering and clanking like its gonna fall apart like when I tried start it that one time, the thing is purring like a kitten. I just stand there and stare. Duncan doesn't notice me cause he's elbows deep in the thing adjusting this and that.

I finally snap out of it and walk over to the contraption. I put my hand out and rest it on top of the motor. It's just thrumming away as pretty and smooth as can be. Duncan looks up at me like he knows he did something wrong and just then the motor quits.

"Duncan? What did you do?"

"Im sorry. Just wanted to see if the fuel mix was right"

"No, I mean how on earth did you start this thing so soon? And why is it running so good?"

"Well, I reseated the injector on the carb and then…"

I interrupted him, "No, I mean….how in the…

nevermind. It runs great!"

"Thanks!" he beams.

"No, thank you….you just saved me, I dunno, a month of wrenching on this thing. You're a genius"

"Well, technically I am. They tested my IQ once and I think it was 280 but that was a while ago"

I have no idea if that's a genius IQ or not but it sounds like a big number and the kid sure seems like a genius judging by the way that motor was running. Then it hits me. He must be one of those gifted type people that do one thing really, really good. Somehow, I don't believe this even though it was my own thought. So I ask him:

"You always been good with motors?

"Uh. Not really. I never worked on one". But,

Chuck this is technically an engine, not a motor. Great. I knew it. I handed this kid a wrench and he coulda stripped every bolt on the motor. But, he didn't. He got it running. Perfect. First time.

"Never?"

He swallows and looks scared again.

"No Sir"

"Drop the sir bit. Duncan, how could you possibly have got this thing running when you have never worked on a motor before?"

"Um. I dunno. I just looked at it and figured it out. It's kinda simple and it just makes sense, I guess"

Just makes sense. It's simple. Of course. Why didn't I think of that. I tell the kid forget it and thank him again. I'm pretty sure giving him a beer is outta the question so I offer him a Coke to celebrate. He accepts with a shy smile and chugs some down. He kinda pulls himself up pokes out his skinny chest and lets loose with a full blast, award winning belch that would make the winner of a hot dog eating contest proud. I mean this thing just kept brapping out and I'm staring in amazement and then I can't stop laughing. He wraps it up with a nice flourish at the end and starts giggling along with me. Before we know it we both got tears streaming out of our eyes and my belly starts hurtin from laughin so hard. The laughter trickles down to a few giggles and I let out a little burp and we almost get going again. My belch is nowhere near as impressive so the laughter finally winds down. The kid looks at me with a goofy smile and I smile back. Just then is when Duncan and me became fast friends.

Now you might be sittin there thinking no normal man is gonna really be friends with a kid. Unless maybe he's got them pedalistic thoughts capering around in his head like some psycho clown. Well, I'm here to tell you it can happen. I dunno. Duncan's dad didn't seem too interested in him and his mom was, well…a mom, so maybe I was a father figure. You know my story about kids so maybe he was the kid I never had. It could have been either or both, but it was more than that too. We were real friends. We talked and laughed and rode my contraption around the neighborhood, which thanks to Duncan actually works now, and even watched football together on my crappy little TV in the garage. Those cool fall days with the door open and us just kicked back on lawn chairs yelling at the QB were good. That's how Duncan got interested in stats. The game was a mystery to him at first. He had no idea if the quarterback was throwing a homerun or making a foul shot, so I explained football to him. If you know football and ever tried to tell someone who doesn't know how the game works, then you know how frustrating it can be. Kinda like describing the color blue to a blind man. Not with Duncan, though. One weekend he didn't know football and the next he was spouting off stats and rules and calls I'd never even heard of. One day, the Bucs were beating the feathers off Philly and in the middle of an intentional grounding call he jumps up and starts going off about how the QB was outta the pocket. I'm looking at Mr. Geek-a-matic like I just discovered some new species and tell him just chill, the call was good, he was in the pocket the whole time.

"No way" he says

"Yes, way. See, watch the replay…."

Just then the other coach throws the flag to dispute the call. Sure enough, after some wrangling, the call gets taken back. Wow. My respect-o-meter jumps up a notch. Respect for myself that is. I turned the nerdiest kid on the block into a sports nut. And one who actually knows a bad call when he sees it.

It goes on like this for a while. Fall turns to winter and winter turns into a new year. Sometime along the way, I went down to Duncan's house and introduced myself. I figgered if the kid was gonna hang out at my house then maybe his parents might wanna have a get-to-know-ya. I guess they didn't. They were polite enough, I suppose, but certainly not warm. Or inviting. I spent the whole time on the front porch. I said I hope you don't think anything strange about me and Dunc hangin out. (after a while he started to like it when I called him Dunc. Guess his dad only ever called him Duncan and it's a bit of a stuffy name, tell the truth.) I told them he's wicked smart and he got my contraption not just running, but rolling and working just like it's sposed to. His mom just said oh that's nice and his dad just said send him home if he gets to be a pest. Just like that. Oh sure, take our kid as long as he's not pesky. Sheesh. Nobody even asked what I did for a living. Not that I do anything at all. I was tired once and I liked it so much I re-tired. Guess they figgered out that since my old pickup only leaves the drive when I'm out of food. Or beer. Or smokes. But they didn't even ask what I did before I joined the ranks of the formally useful. Mom, I can understand. Women don't much care what you do unless they want into your wallet, but that's a pretty standard question for a man. Oh well. If they don't mind me and Dunc hanging out, then all the better. I said nite and mosied on back home and never set foot on their porch again. Until the morning I had to tell them where Dunc went and that he was prolly never coming back.

Superbowl Sunday came up and and Dunc and me were sittin there watching our two least favorite teams make a mess of it. I swear, how these teams get this far is a mystery to me. During one of those stupid commercials, that are sposed to be witty, I glanced over at Dunc. He was starting to grow into himself and fill out a bit. His mom got him contacts which dropped the nerd factor down a bit. His hair was a bit long, the way kids wear it these days, but he was starting to look less like a geek and more like a regular kid. A far cry from the little doofus that walked up my driveway half a year ago. Dunc notices me staring at me and quips:

"Take a picture, it'll last longer"
"Didn't your dad ever teach you to respect your elders?" I come back.

"Yea, but he never said anything about the ancient ones"

"That's a nice way to talk to a guy who invites you over to watch the big game"

"Don't make me get up, Chuck. Upchuck… hahah"

This goes on a bit, like it usually does. Just 2 guys ribbin each'n other. Difference is I'm pushing 40. Ok 50. Alright 70, and he's 12. Whatever, it's just good fun. Still, something about Dunc is naggin at the back of my mind. It's dark and dusty in there, so I turn my attention back to this crappy game. The team that scored the least points lost, like they always do and then, amid all the hoopla and Gatorade spilling going on the tube, it dawns on me. Duncan is wearing a watch. He never wears one. I comment on this now obvious fact.

"Nice watch, Dunc. You get that for Christmas?"

I know he didn't cause he gave me the whole rundown. A telescope, one of those infernal game boxes, some clothes. No watch under the tree. So my naturally nosy self is thinking maybe Dunc finally got himself a girl and she gave it to him as a go-steady present. Wrong. My, my. how wrong I turned out to be.

Guitily, he mumbles, "I found it by the soccer field"

I detect the guilty tone and say,

"Did you turn it in to the lost and found?"

"No, they don't have one"

"Oh well, finders keepers." I could give a rat's patooty about some rich kid's lost watch, but something is amiss here.

"Can I see?"

"Uh…"

I get up on my creaky pins and have a closer looksee. This

is no ordinary watch. It's a dull, satiny, gunmetal gray with a weird little ring around where the dial should be and there's no dial at all. No digital readout either. Where you would expect it to give you the info it's made for, there's about a paragraph of strange writing. Not even writing, really. More like symbols. I start feeling dizzy and think maybe I had one beer too many, which makes no sense cause I only had four during the whole game. One for each quarter. Ok, five. I had one during the halftime show, too. Still, even five beers over three hours is nothing for this old pickle barrel. I glance away from the watch and the dizziness goes away for a sec, I swivel my eyes back to that dial that isn't a dial and the world gets fuzzy again. Ok, I say to myself. You're no spring chicken anymore. Hell, who am I foolin? This chicken is almost ready to cross the road. Still, this is a new twist even for my old gray matter. Duncan sees that things aren't quite right with me and he puts his other hand over the watch. The world stutters back into focus and I tell Dunc,

"That's one strange watch buddy"
He looks away.

"Dunc? What is that thing?"

"I'm not exactly sure, but watch this. Just don't get too close"

He stands up and holds his arm straight out. A vibration starts that I can feel way back in my fillings and Dunc's whole arm start to get blurry. Now I realize that it's not my vision, but that his arm is actually blurry. Like it's an out of focus photograph. Then the little ring over the face, or whatever it is, starts to spin. Slowly at first then picking up speed. It goes faster and faster until it's just a blur. Then it lifts completely off from the watch and hovers about a foot above his wrist and starts spinning on the other axis until it looks like a ball. What happens next, I will never forget in the few short years I have left. The ring moves up and starts orbiting his head like some weird little satellite. Then Duncan starts blurring. I hold up my own hand and it doesn't look blurry. It's just the kid. He's going out of focus and he has this faraway look in his eyes. I scream his name and his eyes focus on me just enough. He drops his arm, the little ring flies back onto the watch like nuthin happened and we're just standing there staring at each other. I have a pretty good idea that my heart is going to fly right out of my chest and fall on the dirty garage floor any second. No problem, Max would prolly lick it clean with his rough tongue, the little mooch, but seriously I feel like I'm gonna at least blow a valve. Neither happens and I slowly catch my breath. Not an easy task after decades of a two packa day habit, but I do manage to get my heartbeat out of the red zone.

"I think it belongs to an alien." he whispers
I'm speechless. In all my long, tiresome years, I have never seen anything like that and I immediately know he's right.

"You have to get rid of it. Lets go call National Geographic or Fox News or something. It's dangerous"

"No. It's my destiny"

"Are you crazy? That thing made you all blurry. You were...I dunno...disintegrating or something"

"No, It's like I'm visiting their world. They want me to come there. They said I'm the most intelligent human they've ever encountered"

"Duncan. They want to have you for lunch. We're calling somebody"
I grab his arm to pull him into the house and he yanks away from me.

"No."

"Please Duncan. Let an expert look at it. You're just a kid. Yeah, a smart one, but you have no idea what that thing does. It could kill you"

He seems to calm down a bit and says

"Ok you're right"

I guide him into the house and pick up the phone. Used to be you could hit the receiver button a few times and get an real human (who even spoke English) to get you a number, but nowadays you gotta talk to some stupid recording. I thought a second.

"Who do you think we should call"

Duncan looks at me and says he's gonna call the only place who really knows what to do and stretches his arm out again. The watch does it's little trick and the ring is orbiting his head again.

"Duncan! NO!"

The ring picks up speed, going around and around his head. The way my stupid mind works, I'm thinking that thing's gotta be doin at least 20,000 rpms and if it breaks its orbit, he's definitely gonna need stitches. The little part of my brain that does all the important thinking pipes up and informs me that stitches are the least of your worries when you start disintegrating, which is exactly what's happening to Duncan. Like some cheap special effect in a bad movie, the kid is going blurry from head to toe. I'm feeling befuddled with that ceaseless vibration, which is now thrumming through my whole body, and I know my heart is going way too fast. I lurch forward to try and get him to drop his arm or something, anything to stop what's happening and there's a blinding flash of light, a huge boom that makes my ears ring like the mortars at Pusan, and then everything starts to go black. The last thing I see before the blinds close all the way is the little gunmetal ring hit the floor and bounce away.

The phone is ringing and ringing cause I never did get an answering machine to make the thing shut up. Why should I? Nobody calls but mushmouthed salesmen who want a slice of my measly pension check. The annoying electronic warble continues until I drag myself up and start to realize what happened. Realize?? Hell, I don't have a clue what happened. I'm sitting upright on the floor and then the memory of what I saw hits me.

"Duncan?" I yell "Dunc? You still here?"

Even before the words leave my lips, I know he's gone. A sadness like I never felt, not even when that witch got on her broom and left me, drops on me like a moldy blanket. But the phone is still ringing so I go to answer it. I have a feeling I know who it is and when I pick it up I say,

"Mrs. Seffner." Duncan's mom

"Hello Mr. Hampton, can you please send Duncan home? It's getting late"

"Um. He's not here" Not lying. Yet.

Silence "Oh. Well if you see him, please tell him to come right home"

"Sure thing" Right. As soon as I build my multiplexdemodulator and beam him back.

"Ok. Thanks. Bye"

"Bye"

I don't know which is worse. The worry I heard in her voice or the fact that I just watched her twelve-year old boy disintegrate to an alien world. Or get eaten. Or worse. Ok. Get a handle old man. People don't just evaporate thanks to weird watches found by a soccer field. Of course not, how silly. Jeez. I thought for sure I was gonna skip the whole oldtimers disease and just die of something simple, like cancer. Guess not. Senile. Crap. Seems easy enough to convince myself until I notice the little gunmetal ring on the floor. I walk over and pick it up. Instantly I feel the vibration in my fillings again. Fainter this time, but it's there. I throw the cursed thing across the room, it bounces off the wall, rolls back and bumps into my shoe. A sigh, ok, a whimper escapes my lips and I pick it up and slide it into my pocket.

Even half asleep I can tell from the cadence of the banging on the door that it's the police. Only a cop can knock that way. They must have a training course on how to rattle people just by knocking. I stumble to the door and open it in my skivvies with my hair sticking up at crazy angles. I'm sure I cut the perfect image of the murderous pedomaniac.

"Mr. Hampton?"

"That's right"

"Do you know Duncan Seffner?"

"I do"

"Have you seen him today?"

"No" lying is easier than you think. Even to the police. Especially when you're lying about aliens eating your best little buddy.

He glances past me into the house, his eyes already scanning for evidence. Max is curling his tail around my bare leg, angling for a way out.

"We understand that you and Duncan spent a lot of time together"

"That's right"

"Uh Huh. Why?"

"We were...I mean we're friends"

"Uh huh. Friends, huh?"

Max makes his move and tears out past Sherlock Holmes. He doesn't even notice. Thanks. Great. What if he goes up a tree? You gonna climb your man in blue rump up there and get him down? Didn't think so.

"Mind if we come in and take a look around?"

"I got a choice?"

"Yep. You can let us come in, or we can go away and get a warrant while you hide the body, and then we'll come in anyway, find the trace evidence, and then you won't even be good enough to be Bubba's wife. In fact, when those guys get done with you, there probably won't be any trace evidence left of you. They don't much like child molesters on the inside"

I swing the door wide and step aside.

"Mind if I go get decent"

"I don't think that's possible, but I'm not really interested in seeing much more of your skinny old legs. Karl, go with the man to get some clothes on."

They rummaged around in my house for a long time. Poked around the garage. Left. Reminded me not to leave town. Persons of interest never get to go see points of interest out of town. Came back. Left again. Meanwhile, everyday when I woke up I looked at the little gunmetal ring. It still made me dizzy, but every morning I put it in the pocket of my britches and carried it around with me. Every night I took it back out and set it on my nightstand. I'm not a religious man. Some are when they come back from killing the little yellow guys. Not me. I figger any God that lets that go on hasn't read his own bible. But I prayed for the first time in my life. I prayed that little man was safe, wherever he was. I prayed that my mind got the best of me and it never even happened, but I knew better; I saw it happen. The all-timers never did kick in, although would have been a blessing in itself, to just forget. But I couldn't. My screams when I woke up tangled in sweat soaked sheets in the middle of the night wouldn't let me forget. Those screams, along with the newspaper articles and the Amber alerts and the neverending investigation wouldn't let me forget. All that stuff also got me the stares from everyone that I probably deserved. No, I didn't kill him and bury him in the backyard, but I let him go and it all amounts to the same thing doesn't it? He's gone and I did nothing to stop it from happening.

I'm an old man but I'm not a used up man yet. I like to think I've always been a man of integrity, and true to that, I screwed up my courage and headed down to Duncan's house. Not before I made my decision. It wasn't an easy decision, but not nearly as hard as this short walk down the block and the conversation that I plan to have with Dunc's parents. I trudge up the porch steps like the old fart that I am and knock on the door. Mrs. Seffner opens the door and just stares at me.

Scathingly, she says, "You have a lot of nerve coming here"

"I know where Duncan went"

"What? Oh my God, tell me. Please! Is he ok?"
She starts crying and Mr. Seffner comes running out. I never had a liking for the guy. Didn't really dislike him either. I was just kinda neutral about him and thought he should maybe spend some more time with his kid. Hell, it woulda been nice if he just noticed Duncan once in a while. Maybe if he did, the poor kid would have evaporated at home, where he should have, and I wouldn't be standing

here doing what I'm about to do. That's nice. I'm turning into such a bitter old turd. I gotta do what I gotta do cause I loved…still love Duncan and it's the right, hell the only thing to do.

Mr Seffner barks "Whats going on here"

"He says he knows where Duncan is"

"My God, man, tell us"

I take a deep breath and relay the whole story to them. Of course they don't believe a word of it and are now certain I'm a crazy old child killer. So I reach into the pocket of my baggy old pants and pull out the ring. I feel it vibrating and tickling the end of my fingers. I hold it up so they can see it and then tip my head back and swallow it. I figgered out a while ago that there wasn't enough power left in the thing or maybe I needed the rest of it to make it work. Then the mental gears kicked into high and I remembered something Duncan said about energy transference in relation to the hydrogen conversion tank I cobbled together and he made work the way it's sposed to. So every day, I hooked up the little ring to the conversion unit and charged it up. And every day the vibration got stronger. Then one day I held the ring long enough to see my fingers get blurry. Just a little, but enough to know it was working. So everyday it went on the charger, and finally I just left it hooked up charging twenty four-seven. I knew it was ready this morning because when I went out to the garage, the conversion unit was blurry and wavering like the road in the distance on a hot day. I also figgered that if I swallowed the thing, maybe it would swallow me. Guess I was right.

One Seffner screamed like a little girl and The other Seffner fainted out cold as I started to get blurry and the world that

I knew disappeared forever in the shimmering, blurry light of a thousand ancient suns. I never even heard the boom.

THE KILLER

It was his first job and he was, understandably, nervous. The fact that he had to do it at night didn't help, but he supposed, this sort of thing was best done in the dark, after most normal people were tucked away in bed. Less chance of being seen that way even though his handiwork would be evident as soon as the sun rises. He was prepared for the most part. He studied his subject, mapped out his route, and even did a dry run. But how does one really prepare for this sort of unpleasantness? He hoped it wouldn't be too messy. It likely would be and he had made plans for that too. He purchased a pair of snug fitting gloves and just the right garb to protect his street clothes. He was as ready as he would ever be so he locked his door and hit the street.

He walked down the glistening sidewalk, fresh and slick from the recent rain. It seemed the only people out at this early morning hour long before the dawn were the creatures of the night that haunted the doorways and alleys. Cheap whores and beggars for the most part, but he did see others like himself. Purposeful men and women on their way to do important and perhaps unpleasant, but necessary, things like him. He descended into the subway station and was obliged to step over a bum sleeping in a pile of garbage. Disgust filled him and he thought that if things went well tonight, he might even do some freelance work on his own. Clean this city up a bit. He knew that was risky and went against everything he had studied, but this was his town and really, who would complain? Confident in his future altruism, he forgot the bum and picked up a bit of a spring in his step. This was going to go well, he could feel it.

The subway whooshed into the station and he had to jog to get on before the automatic door denied his entry. His momentum and the forward lurch of the train bumped him into a fellow passenger and he mumbled a quick city "scuseme" and plopped into a seat. He glanced around the mostly empty car and spied a discarded newspaper. He felt a twinge of annoyance at the careless rider who left the paper behind. Everything it it's place and place for everything, he always said. That philosophy was good enough for his dad and it was good enough for him. It was also that attention to detail that brought him to this point in his life. You had to be detail oriented in this type of work or you just made a mess of things and that was not good. He retrieved the paper, rearranged the loose sections in the correct order and began reading.

The well-dressed gentleman that he bumped into stepped towards him and asked if he could read a part of the paper that he just so carefully rearranged. This guy would probably just throw the section down, forgotten, on the seat when his stop slowly rolled into view. Well, perhaps not. He cut a good figure in his black overcoat and obviously expensive briefcase. He gave the man a section without a second glance.

At the next stop, the only other passenger, an old black woman, shuffled off the train, the doors closed and the train continued on its endless loop through the city. He glanced around the almost empty car and noticed the well-dressed man staring at him over the paper. The guy was probably sizing him up for some gay fantasy. No matter, he would be off at the next stop. He read on about the usual Washington foolishness and ignored the guy. Better to not encourage him with eye contact. He stood when he felt the train slowing as it approached his station and the other man made as if he was getting off too. Great, he thought, now I'll have to fend off some disgusting advance in a lonely subway station. This is exactly the sort of distraction he did not need on such an important day. No matter, he had his own special way of dealing with situations like this. Just as the station platform came into view the man reached forward to hand him back the newspaper section he borrowed. Well he thought, even if he is homosexual, he's a neat one. The garbage truck driver felt a moment of confusion, then pain then nothing at all as the well-dressed killer expertly slipped the knife between his fourth and fifth ribs.

SOMEPLACE

He walked alone down the long dark hallway. It smelled here and it was cold and he was scared. This was an ugly place; full of stale misery and rotted dreams. He wondered for the hundredth time what he was even doing in the place. Especially alone. The answer, as usual, never came and he walked on, things crunching under his shoes in the dark. The place was old. Older than he was by a lifetime or two. There were old things here too. They crouched in the dark and brooded in unexpected places that would give you a fright when you saw them. At least at first they did. He'd been here so many times that he was used to just about everything. Except just being here at all. That still gave him a fright. Partly because the place did that to you and partly because he didn't know why he kept coming back.

He was always afraid of rats when he came but he never saw one alive. There were plenty of dead ones, but even they looked like the place: dried up hollow shells. It was as if they gave up and died because it was just too much trouble to do otherwise. He understood how they felt. This place siphoned off your spirit one tentative footstep at a time. Once, he found a dead dog on a lower level. It too was mummified and yet he had been here the week before and there was no sign of it at the time. He didn't ponder the possible meaning of this because if he did, he might never come back. Especially alone.

He always came alone and no one else came here. He was certain of it. He knew because he left things behind and they were always in the same place. There was dust on the floor but the only footprints in it were his. Size twelve and the tread pattern slightly worn. He wondered if he died here would anyone find him? Surely someone would but the question was when. Would he also be a dried up husk silently mouthing his misery and desolation? Probably. But he was not going to die in here mostly because it would be poetic. He never was a poetic man and his reasons for coming here weren't either. He just came because he did and asked himself why and that was that.

He glanced out a grimy, cracked window and saw that the sky was lightening. He turned on his heel and headed for a passage back out into the real world. On his way, he dropped something on the floor that he knew would be exactly where it fell when he came back next week.

FALL TO PIECES

I don't know if I'll be able to finish this story. I'm very tired and something is eating me piece by piece. Both my legs are gone and I only have two fingers left-one on each hand. That's all I normally type with anyway, but when they're gone I don't know what I will type with; my nose maybe. It's served me well so far, but it's likely too large to press the keys with any accuracy. Even if I could type with my nose, it's getting difficult to sit at the computer without my legs.

I will try my best to get everything on paper before I'm completely gone. I feel that someone should know. Even though I have no family left and precious few friends, none of whom actually stay in touch with me, I should at least let the creepy old landlord know. Mr. Smolensk is an ancient, smelly thing that always has a booger either perched defiantly on the outside of his nostril, or smeared through his thin, greasy hair. I guess he picks his nose and then smooths his hair flat and in the process transfers the hideous green things to his pate. Or maybe they migrate from his nose to his hair while he's sleeping. Either way, boogers or not, he is my landlord and I'm a firm believer in keeping one's obligations. Or at least offering a viable reason as to why I am unable.

I should start at the beginning. Or I suppose you could call it the end. I woke up early one Saturday morning. I always wake up early. I don't have much to look forward to, especially on the weekend when there's no work and only laundry and tidying up, but I'm up with the sun anyway. I got up this particular Saturday and went about my morning ritual of shower, shave, breakfast and quick look at the morning paper. I still believe in reading words formed by droplets of ink on a piece of real paper. Not that all the electronic miracles aren't exactly that, it's just that if people go about the trouble of printing the thing, the least I can do is read it. I found an article of some interest so I folded the page over for easier reading, grabbed my mug and headed out to the porch to finish the story. It was a clear, bright day already and promised to be pleasant enough for some gardening later or maybe a walk. I sat down in my wicker chair, pleasantly content in my solitude, and put my feet up on the cassock. That's when I noticed the nail was gone from my right big toe. I stared for a moment, the paper forgotten on my lap, in that manner when you can't quite believe what you are seeing. When that happens to me I get a sinking feeling that the Alzheimers is setting in. My father ended up with it and his father died "senile" too. Which is, of course, what they called it before giving it a fancy name and vainly trying to find a cure. My mother, luckily, didn't catch it. She was, unluckily, run over by a train. Maybe there would have been a chance for her to end up senile, but a Southern-Pacific locomotive traveling at forty made her diagnosis forever a mystery. I stared at the pink spot where my toenail should have been and thought how strange because there was no pain at all. If you've ever ripped a nail off of your toe or finger I think you'll agree that it's not something that goes without notice. I set the paper on the small table beside me and bent forward for a closer look. Yep. The nail was definitely gone. I touched the smooth, pinkish skin and the nerve endings there were either asleep or dead because there was no pain. In fact, there was no feeling at all. I grunted quizzically and looked around the floorboards of the porch for the missing nail. It couldn't have fallen through the cracks because there were none. The porch had been painted so many times that the boards were fused together by coat after coat of white paint. Probably deadly with lead too. I set the paper aside and went inside, my eyes scanning the floor all the while. I looked in the bathroom, checking the tub and behind the commode. I have no idea how my big toenail could have made it behind the commode, but I'm thorough if nothing else. I scoured my sheets and turned all my dirty socks inside out. No sign of even a clipped nail, let alone one in its entirety. I stood in my bedroom, one dirty sock dangling from my hand looked again at my toe, sans nail. It was vaguely disturbing and I resolved to set an appointment with the local doctor on Monday morning. Not that I trusted that old quack to accurately take my temperature, but what choice did I have? This is a small town and the options are narrow. It was either him or the veterinarian. I hid the thought of my missing nail with the aid of a pair of socks-clean ones-and went about my day.

The next morning started out as a direct repeat of the one before. Until, while on the commode, I looked down and saw that all the toenails on my right foot were gone. An unpleasantly cold feeling gripped my bowels and I thought I needn't worry anymore about Alzheimers. I was obviously riddled with cancer. Or some other equally devastating illness. Why else would all my toes suddenly divest themselves of their nails? I finished on the commode, and vainly went through the process of searching for the missing nails, but they proved as elusive as the first one. I ended up in the living room, my foot up on the edge of the table staring at my toenail-less foot. I compared it to the other foot. A mirror image with the obvious exception. There appeared to be no indication that the other nails were weak or brittle or loose. That was at least something. And, there was no pain. Another something to hold on to. I checked my fingernails and they too seemed fine. I got up, retrieved the phone book, and looked up Dr. Brantly's number. He was, of course, closed, but I left a message on the machine requesting an immediate appointment in the morning. Not an emergency, I explained, but urgent nonetheless. Feeling a bit better having reached out to a professional, albeit an inept one in my opinion, I went about my day as best as one can with only five toenails.

Monday morning came early and the phone rang. Dr. Brantly explained that he couldn't see me right away as his receptionist/medical assistant/wife was under the weather and he would need to attend to all the day's tasks himself. Why on earth I would see a doctor who couldn't even treat his own wife crossed my mind, but as I mentioned, I had few options. Besides, he continued, it's not an emergency right? And what is the nature of your complaint anyway? I started to explain and thought a malady such as this might be better described in person. I stared down at my foot in horror and mumbled that I was feeling better anyway and would call tomorrow if something changed. It was a good thing the doctor hung up first because my shaking hand failed to get the phone back on its cradle and it crashed to the floor. I gripped the edge of the phone table and stared blankly at the four toes left on my right foot. I wiggled them and they all functioned perfectly even without nails but where the big toe should have been leading the wiggle was nothing but empty space. I lurched over to the couch and sat down hard. There was no need to limp because there was no pain. I stared at the spot where my big toe should have been and it was as smooth as the rest of my foot. It didn't even look amputated: there was no blood, no scar and no toe. I rubbed my finger over the nearly round patch of skin and it felt as if I was touching someone else, in other words there was no feeling at all. I suddenly felt woozy as some people do when they see blood or a broken bone. Sweat popped out my forehead, my eyes rolled up in my head and my brain decided that right then and there would be a good time to shut down for a bit.

I'm not sure how long I was out, but the shadows had moved to the other side of the room. I wiped my hand across my face and it came away damp with greasy sweat. I stood up to check the time and fell flat on my face. I heard a sickening crunch, my eyes went blurry and my brain threatened to shut down again. I reached up and felt my broken nose and the excruciating pain instantly squelched any possibility of another faint. I rolled over on my back and managed to get myself up into a sitting position. I stared with utter horror at my left foot, which was now also devoid of nails. This minor spectacle somehow kept me from noticing the absence of my entire right foot for a few precious seconds. When my eyes swiveled in that direction they lingered long enough to register the stump of my shin and promptly rolled right back up in my head. Just before I passed out, I heard, rather than felt, my head thump solidly on the oaken floor.

When I came around it was fully dark in the house. I layed still for a bit while waves of nausea rolled in time with the throbbing of my head and my nose. I marveled at how the pain came and went with each heartbeat. Funny, I thought, how the human body works so well together. I assumed, correctly, that I now had a concussion in addition to a broken nose and a missing foot. The thought of my missing foot jolted me and I sat up too fast. Bright flashes of light sparkled around the periphery of my vision and I bit down on my lip to keep from passing out yet again. I took a deep breath, closed my eyes and slowly the sparkly lights went away. I looked down in the gloom at where my right foot should have been and saw a horrific symmetry that was all wrong. My mind refused to accept the undeniable fact that both feet were now missing. I rolled over with a groan and crawled to the couch. As I pulled myself up on the couch I latched onto the certainty that I was dreaming. To consider any other possibility would surely result in my mind snapping like an overstretched rubber band. I curled up in a fetal position and simply closed my eyes.

I dreamed I was eating blue crabs with my dad. He loved those things. He would take me in the summer down a dirt road by the bay where an old man sold crabs off of his houseboat. The place was always pungent with the smell of salt air, fish, sweat and cigar smoke. I loved it. It had the smell of men working hard by the water and to me, that was one of the sure smells of summer. There in the crab man's crowded floating shack, my dad would pull out a bottle of whiskey and tell dirty jokes and laugh and clap the old guy on the back and haggle over the crabs. He would tell me later it was to get a better price or a baker's dozen, but I knew better. He enjoyed the old man and his smells and his lifestyle. My dad always said he wished he could be a sailing man, a man of the sea. I guess I didn't really believe that but the time spent with the crab man made it seem not only true, but possible. In my dream we rattled down the dirt road with a bucket of live crabs on the backseat. When we got home my dad prepared a large boiling pot of water and pungent spices. One by one, he dropped the live crabs into the boiling water. He explained that they didn't feel any pain. How he knew this was beyond me and I wasn't so sure. I felt a bit of pity for the ugly creatures, not too much though because they were so tasty. We sat down at the table, newspapers spread out to catch the shells and drippings and began snapping claws and shells. My dad selected the largest crab in the bunch and prepared to amputate a claw. The crab suddenly awoke from it's boiling water and spice induced slumber and neatly clipped off my dad's index finger. He screamed and I screamed and the crabs started pouring out the bowl and swarming my dad. Within seconds he was covered with fourteen angry blue crabs (he had managed to get not one, but two baker's dozen from the crab man). Of course, they were no longer blue but red from the boiling pot. I tried to pull them off my dad and then he turned into a giant crab. I stared into the hideous gaping maw of it's weird, hairy mouth and it bit my head off.

I awoke on the couch to a scream and realized that it came from my own mouth. I layed still for a bit allowing the dream to dissipate. I looked out the sun filled window and my thoughts drifted to my dad. I felt an unexpected sadness. I remembered a time when he cut off the tip of his finger with a power saw. The doctors sewed the tip back on but he was told there would never be a nail on that finger. Well, my dad set out to eat as many crabs as he could over the next few months and damn if that nail didn't grow back. Something about the regenerative power of the crabs transferred to him and he actually regrew that which the doctors claimed would not. It always baffled me how he had the instinct to do that. Ours was not a great relationship, but he was my dad, and at that moment I missed him dearly. I also missed my feet and the thought of their absence mostly erased the memories of my dad. Except the instinct of renegration that he had. Maybe if I ate some crabs my feet would grow back. It seemed absurd but when your feet mysteriously disappear, you gain a whole new view of the ridicuous.

I sat up on the couch and stared at the flat material of my pants that should have been filled with my right leg. The rubber band inside my mind snapped. I didn't pass out again, which would have been a blessing, but rather sat there in utter disbelief. I felt the material of my pants, and yep, no leg. I did the only thing that made sense. I slid off the couch, not too gracefully I might add, and began to crawl to the hall closet. It took a few minutes. The house isn't large but even fifteen feet is a journey for a one legged man. I thought if only I had a peg for my leg. Arrr, a pirate I could be. A maniacal laugh briefly giggled out and I squelched it. If I started laughing now I wouldn't stop until I asphyxiated myself with it. Maybe not such a bad way to go; laughing to death. Gotta be better than going to pieces like this. The laugh threatened again and I set my thoughts squarely on the hall closet. In it I would find not a pegleg but an old crutch I saved from when I gave my ankle a nasty twist a few years ago. I finally got to the closet and pulled myself up on my remaining stump. I opened the door and rummaged through winter coats and things I bought and never used and forgot about. Ah ha. There in the back was the crutch. I pulled it out and set it under my right armpit.

It still wasn't an easy go. My footless stump made for precarious balancing and on my way to the bathroom I took a nasty tumble. The fall turned up the volume on my concussion and a wave of nausea flowed over me. I took a deep breath and slowly dragged myself back up. I finally made it to the bathroom where leaned against the wall and unbuttoned my trousers and let them fall to the floor. I looked at the place where my right leg lived for the last thirty three years with a detached curiosity. It was a blank area and slightly ovoid in shape. I dropped my underwear and marveled at how my testicles swung free in the direction of my missing limb. I realized my bladder was full so I hobbled over to the commode and urinated. For a long time. When I was done, I glanced in the mirror and saw the horror that I had become. Another mooring line in my mind let loose. I had to do something.

I hobbled to the kitchen in search of my car keys. The hospital. Yes, I must check myself in. The emergency room wouldn't do. No blood, no contusions, no emergency. Specialists were what I needed. Highly trained men with needle and thread. But what would they sew back on to me? You need to supply whatever body part you want sewn back on and I had none to offer. I didn't look for my leg, or my feet, but I had a feeling they were nowhere to be found. It's not like a leg is something you can easily misplace. If it was around surely I would have seen it. Then I could walk (or hobble) to the specialists and politely request that they sew it back on. This line of thinking would get me nowhere. My appendages were gone and that was that. The doctors would simply have to figure something else out. A prosthetic or two or three perhaps. Or maybe take two crabs and call them in the morning.

I got my car keys and headed to the door when I realized I had no leg with which to press the accelerator. Screw it, I thought. I'll use my left leg for brakes and gas. I got as far as the couch and suddenly felt very tired. I slept all night, but a broken nose, a concussion and missing limbs tend to knock the wind out of your sails. A pirate joke danced around in what was left of my mind like a drooling lunatic and I ignored it. I made my way to the couch and plopped down. I put my remaining leg up on the table and promised myself just a quick nap to get my energy back.

I instantly drifted off with a spiraling feeling that descended into a dreamless but fitful sleep. I woke feeling less rested than when I began. I also woke with a realization that you may have already had. It took me some time to come to this fact, but you have to understand that I was a bit distracted and not thinking quite clearly. My body parts were disappearing while I was asleep. Where did they go? I had no real idea; only a sneaking suspicion that something was eating me. I knew it didn't make sense because there was no bite marks or blood, but what other conclusion could I draw? Both my legs were now gone and four fingers on my right hand. The pirate jokes no longer applied and the last anchor in my mind let go with a snappy twang. I was till lucid enough, even with my mind drifting around in my head like a balloon with no string, to realize that the decision to go to the hospital was out of my hands. I couldn't drive a car with no legs and besides I only had one crutch. I also realized that if I fell asleep again I would wake up much less of a man than I already was.

That was when I decided I better do something to keep myself awake so I started committing these words to paper. It was a real pain in the ass to get to the computer. I mean that literally. I had to pull myself along with my arms, my derierre dragging and bumping along the floor. I racked my balls pretty good too. That feeling made my broken nose feel like a gentle caress. I got to the computer table and managed to mountain climb the chair and take a seat. It's tricky to sit with no legs, let me tell ya, but I got the hang of it and fired up the computer. I set out to document my disintegration and keep myself awake as long as possible in the process. Needless to say, it didn't work. As I typed, the words on the screen began to double, then treble. I set my head on my arm for a moment's rest and drifted off.

Now here I am with no legs and only two fingers. When my arms are gone I will no longer have the capacity to type. You can't really type with your nose. So, to Mr. Smolensk, my landlord, I apologize, but I won't have the rent this month. I hope you understand. It's difficult for a torso to write a check or even count out bills. I could tell you where my wallet is and let you get the money yourself, but frankly I don't want your boogers on my stuff. To my friends, who may or may not read this, screw you for not calling me or visiting. You really made me go to pieces. Ha ha. I'm tired again now so I'll finish this in a bit.

MIDNIGHT AND THE MACHINE

I named the crow Midnight. Not because it came around at the witching hour, or because it was particularly mysterious. The crow itself was a rather unassuming and basically like any other crow. What it did was quite mysterious indeed. I named it Midnight for the same reason people name their black cat Shadow or their black dog, well, Blackie. It was an animal, it didn't care what I called it and, frankly, I couldn't think of anything else. The first time Midnight came to my window wasn't midnight at all; it was shortly past 8pm. I know because I was watching a nonsensical talent show in which contestants with no talent at all performed horribly to the delight of the audience and the scorn of the judges. The crow didn't tap-tap-tap on my window, nor did it cry "nevermore!" Thank God, because it gave me enough of a start as it was. It simply lighted on the sill and stood there with the first piece of the machine that would eventually change, and nearly destroy, my life in its beak.

For the moment, a crow standing on my windowsill was much more interesting than the plodding, endless commercial on the tube hawking some medical miracle that seemed to cause more maladies than it cured. I sat motionless and looked at the bird as it ruffled it's feathers a few times and then gingerly placed something on the sill. Great, I thought. The thing is going to make a nest right outside my window. I imagined the mess of bird crap dripping down the wall and tried to shoo the crow away. It just stood there and cocked its head down at whatever it placed on the sill. I shooed again, and again it looked down. Enough was enough. I got up and walked the few paces to the window expecting the crow to fly off. It just stood there and looked up at me, the flickering TV glinting off one beady eye. It was becoming more than annoying; it was a bit creepy. I rapped my knuckles on the glass and the arrogant thing finally took the hint and winged away.

      "And don't come back" I proclaimed to the empty sill.

I looked to see what nest makings or droppings it left and was surprised to see a small metal gear on the sill. I checked to be sure the crow was relly gone, the last thing I needed was a wild bird trapped in the house, flying into the walls and pooping everywhere. After assuring myself it was indeed gone, I opened the sash. I reached out, picked up the gear and immediately dropped it in revulsion. The small piece of metal was warm to the touch. I didn't know if birds were warm-blooded or not, but even if they were, it was a chilly night and there's no way that little gear should have been anything but cool. Like normal metal should be after being left out in the night air on a stone sill. Still, I was curious so I picked the gear up again. It was still warm. Even more fascinating was the intricacy of the machining. It was perhaps the diameter of a quarter and looked to have at least 25 teeth. On the surface was a delicate filigreed pattern and some very tiny letters. It appeared to be from a different era, almost Victorian, yet it was shiny as if new. I closed the window and walked to the kitchen where there was more light. The words on the surface still eluded me so I rummaged around in the catch-all drawer and fished out a magnifying glass. Through my squint I could finally make out the words N. Eve & R. Moore Machine Company, Phila, Pa. Interesting, but not as much as the woman on the television croaking out the worst version of "Hey Jude" I have ever heard. I tossed the magnifying glass and the gear in the drawer and forgot about it.

Until the next night. I had dozed off in the middle of a game show that asks you to ask a question instead of giving an answer. I awoke with a start when I heard a loud clinking sound. I still had a nearly empty bowl in my lap from my pathetic bachelor's dinner and I thought I had tipped the congealing contents out onto the floor along with my fork. I blinked at the bowl for a second or two before my groggy brain registered that the fork was still firmly installed in the now chilly chili. I heard the clinking noise again and swiveled my eyes towards to window. The hair on the back of my neck rose as I realized the crow was back. It was picking something up from the sill and dropping it. Clink. The crow picked it up again and noticed me noticing it and dropped the thing again. Clink. It cocked its tiny black pellet of eye toward the object and flapped off into the night. Curiosity, of course, got the better of me and I went to retrieve tonight's offering from the crow. It was another gear, warm to the touch and very similar to the other one except that it was a bit larger. I took it to the kitchen to compare it to the other one. I got the other gear from the drawer and laid them side by side on the counter. They were nearly exact and had obviously come from the same place. In fact, not only did they come from the same place, but apparently from right next to each other. The teeth meshed together perfectly. The gray haired game show host was cordially inviting the loser off his stage, and my curiosity was peaked, so I scooped up the gears, walked in the living room and switched off the tube. I opened my laptop, which was sleeping on the table like a lazy cat and examined the gears while I waited for the computer to boot up. The new gear looked to have the same writing on it, but I wanted to be sure so I went back to the kitchen for the magnifying glass. By the time I walked the few steps, the laptop was ready to turn my wishes into commands. I ignored the computer for a moment and raised the magnifying glass to the new gear. Not surprisingly, I saw decorative lines and N. Eve & R. Moore Machine Co., Phila, Pa engraved on the surface. I set the gear and the magnifying glass down and turned to the laptop. I opened my Internet connection and typed in the machine company's name. I didn't really expect to find a result and I wasn't disappointed. The search engine asked me if I meant something else and I said no. I then typed "machine companies in Philadelphia". This time I hit the jackpot with over a quarter of a million results. Never being one to root through endless search results, I scanned the first page and gave up and closed the laptop. I sat looking at the gears for a few minutes pondering where they could have come from. Philadelphia was obviously their origin, but I was states away from there. They looked shiny and new, yet old fashioned. The configuration of the gears reminded me of a watch's inner workings, but they were far too large for a watch. A clock made sense, but then why would they be imprinted with a machine company name and not a clock maker's? I supposed that a machine company could make clock parts. A clock is, after all, a machine that vainly tries to measure the unmeasurable. My mind went round and round trying to figure out where that crow was stealing these things from. It never entered my mind to ask why it was stealing them and leaving them on my windowsill. After what I thought was a few minutes, I put the gears down on the table and got up to stretch. Not getting any younger, I thought, as a straightened out my stiff back. As I squinted out the window at the bright sunlight streaming in, I plopped back on the couch with a grunt. Sunlight? What the hell is the sun doing on in the middle of the night? But, of course, it wasn't night anymore. I looked at the clock on the wall in horror and saw that it was nearly 7 am. I had sat there all night staring at those stupid gears. Not possible, my mind told me. The clock ticked to itself as if telling me whatever you say; I just keep the time, buddy. I must have fallen asleep at some point. Yeah, that was it. I fell asleep on the couch. Holding the gears. Sitting in the same position. I didn't quite convince myself, but I didn't want to consider the idea that I lost eight hours staring at little metal pieces that a crow left for me.

I rushed through my morning ritual, leaving out the caffeine and delaying the nicotine until I was in the car and on my way to the office. The day plodded on like an old man walking up too many stairs and my mind kept drifting back to the gears. Five o'clock finally came and I gathered up my stuff and evacuated my desk. Driving home I pondered stopping for take out, but my impatience to get back and look at the gears won over. I dropped my keys on the counter next to the gears and bent down close to observe them. I looked like an umpire about to make a call, but what I saw instead of a strike was the tiny machine pieces slowly rotating. I blinked my eyes and they were just sitting there; like the inert pieces of metal that they were.

I must be delirious from lack of food, I thought. I tried to remember if I had eaten lunch and the memory eluded me. My stomach grumbled and assured me I had not. I grabbed some cardboard cuisine and threw it in the micro. Five minutes later I was presented with a steaming plate of processed chemicals containing a dash of actual food. I wolfed the mess down and dumped the plastic plate in the trash can. I picked up the gears and went into the living room. I placed them on the table together, with the teeth meshed together. I found that if I placed my finger on the center of one I could slowly spin the other one. I watched in fascination as I rotated the two gears in tandem. I heard a clinking sound and glanced up at the window. The crow was standing there looking at me. This time I had a pretty good idea what the noise was. I got up and went to the window. The crow picked up the object it had just dropped and stood there with a piece of metal in its yellow beak. I looked closely at the crow for a moment. I noticed, for the first time, that it was very shiny. Its feathers were perfectly tucked into each other and had an almost blue sheen to them. The eye that I saw as beady the last two nights now seemed more intense, almost intelligent. It was obviously not afraid of me because it just stood there with its skinny bird legs firmly planted, looking at me as I looked at it. It cocked it's head as if to say "You gonna make me stand here all night or are you gonna open the window?" So I did just that. I had a fleeting thought that I must be losing my mind because I'm having a mental conversation with a bird. The thought went as fast as it came and I slid the window open. For some reason, I was not surprised in the slightest when the crow took flight across my living room and expertly landed on the coffee table next to the gears. It dropped the piece of metal next to the gears, then picked up the larger one. It then carefully placed the gear onto the new piece of metal, which I now saw was a small bracket of sorts with two pegs. I had a sense of deja-vu or rather a sense of destiny fulfilled as the bird then retrieved the other gear and placed it on the remaining peg. It looked at me and then looked at what was no longer random metal parts, but a piece of a machine. I followed its gaze and nearly passed out when I saw that the gears were slowly turning of their own accord. The crow snapped its beak as if in satisfaction and flew past me and out the window. I stood there staring at the tiny gears on their bracket, slowly turning, obviously exactly as they were intended to do. My focus drew in on the object like a focus pull in a movie and my entire world became the machine. I would prefer to say that my mind was turning a million questions at that point, but the truth is my mind was an utter void. There was me, I was sure of that because I could feel the chill air from the open window on my skin, and there was the machine. Aside from man (me) and machine, there was nothing else. Then I snapped out of it. I shivered and turned to close the window. I stopped dead in my tracks and stood staring at the windowsill like a department store dummy. There was another piece of machine on the sill. I was so enraptured by what the crow had done and what the machine was doing that I didn't notice that it had come back with yet another part. As I reached out and retrieved the warm piece of metal, a small cylinder with tiny screws circling it, the crow came back again. It didn't fly into the house this time. It just sat there with its new offering. I took the small velvet bag from its beak and it flew off. I didn't ponder this series of bizarre events much. To consider what was happening too closely surely would end up with a one-way trip to a place with leather restraints, dayrooms with bars and doctors with very large needles. So instead, I did the sensible thing and sat down to figure how to assemble a Victorian machine that a crow was delivering to me piece by piece. I also decided that a crow capable of all this deserved a name. So that night I named him Midnight. I had quite a bit of savings socked away. Why wouldn't I? I was in my thirties, had worked since I was a teenager and I had no wife, no pets, no real friends and certainly no hobbies. I had a tiny rented apartment in a less than great neighborhood, a television to keep me company and cardboard boxes of unhealthy food in the freezer. That kind of lifestyle lends itself very nicely to saving a tidy sum of money. It's a good thing too, because exactly two weeks after the crow brought me the first piece of the machine, I lost my job. Well, I'll be honest with you; I didn't really lose my job. I know exactly where it is, it's just that somebody else is now doing it. And collecting the paycheck. But, that's ok with me. I never liked my job anyway, and besides, I had a much more important job now: finishing the machine. I don't how many more parts it needs, or what it will look like when it's complete, or even what it does. None of that is really important. What's important is that I finish it. It's become quite complicated these last few weeks (months? years? Time has become a wee bit irrelevant lately), almost beautiful in its delicate intricacies. The tiny gears which move by way of levers and pinions and the shiny rotating cylinders and the clear crystal sight glass and the gauge at the top with the strange numbers and the other thousands of parts all working in pure harmony are not almost beautiful, they are gorgeous beyond compare. Midnight was quite busy delivering all the necessary components night and day, one right after the other. He couldn't have gone far to get the pieces because sometimes it's only minutes between deliveries. Other times it was hours. No matter, he brought the parts and I assembled them. Sometimes Midnight would bring a piece and I would be unable to figure out where it went. If he came back and I still hadn't placed the part, he would look at me as if to say "Do I have to do everything around here?" and install the piece in the right place. This went on and on until one night Midnight didn't come. Then another and another. I started to get panicky because it was obvious the machine was not finished yet. How did I know it wasn't finished? It was as obvious as looking at a caterpillar and knowing it too was not finished becoming what it was intended to become. I spent the days and nights by the window waiting for Midnight to come back. I sat there until I could smell myself and my stomach grumbled and gurgled with lack of food. I sat as rain soaked me, ran down the wall and soaked the floor. I sat sleeping upright and I sat with silent tears streaming down my face at the thought of Midnight never coming back and the machine never being complete. Then, one night I heard the flapping of wings and I cried tears of joy as Midnight landed on the sill, a shiny brass key in his mouth. I almost hugged him and then remembered that birds don't have arms. No matter, he flew right past me anyway and landed on the table. His claws clicked on the surface as he walked around the machine tilting his head here, examining a part there. Finally, he inserted the tiny key in a keyhole. Of course. A key goes in a keyhole like a pencil goes in a sharpener like a bolt goes into a nut. Except I knew every inch of that machine and there was no keyhole. Until tonight. After placing the key into the keyhole that was never there, Midnight stepped back and cocked his head at me. Of course I knew what to do. So I walked over to the machine, which had now taken over my coffee table and my life and turned the key. I felt, more than heard, a low rumbling that spoke of a much larger machine than the one that currently held my gaze. The rumbling got more intense, then became audible, and then began rattling the window that Midnight made such productive use of. A small wisp of smoke began to rise from the machine along with a tortured squeal of metal. I could see the machine vibrating and then rattling and then actually bouncing on the table. Parts began to fly off at a dangerous velocity. One shot into the television and the tube exploded in deadly shards of glass. My heart was pounding and an icy finger of fear tickled down my spine. I wasn't afraid for my safety, I was afraid that machine would destroy itself, which is exactly what happened a second later. The thing blew apart in a metal hail of gears and screws and delicate little brass things, all with N. Eve & R. Moore Machine Co. Phila, Pa stamped on them. I know, because I examined every one of them under the magnifying glass. I screamed a guttural "NO!" at the top of my lungs as the world went black and the machine was no more.

I awoke, sweaty and tangled in sheets to Amy shaking me with a worried look on her face.

"Are you ok honey? Did you have a bad dream?"

Olivia poked her head in our room, eyes wide,

"Daddy! You scared me!"

I looked at my beautiful wife, and my little miracle of a daughter and saw they both had the same eyes. I knew this, of course, but it never ceased to amaze me.

"I'm fine, sweeties. Just a bad dream."

Amy said, "Must have been what you ate. No more leftover chili for you before bed. "

"Yeah. No more chili for me. Never again"

HOWEY'S ISLAND

It was the kind of day that sends Northerners flocking South. The sky was the color of faded denim with cotton-ball clouds lazily floating by. This combined with the brilliant sun sparkling off the water and the warm breeze tousling our hair left no doubt that we were exactly in the middle of paradise. There were afternoon storms off on the horizon, but it was early and they were no threat to us. We sat on the rear swim platform of the small, but powerful fishing boat, our feet dangling in the bath-warm sea water. The girls were up front, sunning on the cushions, slathered in oil. The smell of coconut sunscreen drifted through the air along with Reggae quietly dancing out of the speakers. My friend handed me an icy cold bottle of water out of the cooler and I drank half of it down. We clinked our plastic bottles in toast and marveled that it just doesn't get any better than this. As we sat bobbing on the gentle swells and enjoying the moment, I noticed a strip of land with a small beach a few miles off in the bay. I pointed and asked about it, thinking a trip to a seemingly deserted island might be just be icing on the world's best cake. My friend looked at me in a funny way and said we could get a little closer look, but there's no way he was going to try to land us there. He explained that there was a dangerous shallow area where we could get stuck before reaching the little beach. The bottom was covered in razor sharp oyster shells and besides, for some reason, dead fish always washed up there and the place smelled of their floating, rotting corpses. I asked if the place was deserted and he said there used to be a house there and there's still a small cemetery. My interested piqued and I told him to continue.

He told me most of the graves are empty. Some are only partially full. Headstones that read simply Father or Mother or Son or Daughter are common. Some graves have names etched into their thin granite slabs and some graves have partners buried next to them. Some of these say Husband and Wife and one or two say Brother and Sister. There's a even a few that simply read Baby with only one date. Some contain only parts of the anonymous souls interred within, because even if you only have a small part of a person, say an arm or a leg or a head, it must be buried so their tortured soul can rest. Almost all the graves marked Captain are empty because the dearly departed's body has never been found. The sea is an unforgiving mistress and she rarely gives up those who dance too close to her dark, green bosom. Some stones have toppled over from decades of dry winters and wet summers. Weeds and wildflowers are the only memorials to the lost. There are no family members left to maintain nor mourn the lonely and empty graves on this windswept expanse next to the sea. Half a mile down the sandy road and a quarter mile as it curves to the north stands the largest empty grave. A marble edifice to the man who bought this island and made it a gift to his then pregnant wife. It was to be a gift that would provide relaxation and luxury while she waited and then labored to provide him the heir to his fortune. Howard James Williams is etched into the facade of his mausoleum, but Howard James "Howey" Williams is not interred there. Neither is his wife, who wanted nothing more than to please Mr. Howey. I can't say for sure that she died on the island, but I do know that she spent less than one day here.

There's no words chiseled into the marble for his wife or the baby she carried nearly full term, but never delivered. She died like she lived; in the big shadow of her husband, Howey. There's a reason Marty had to go the way she did, just like I suppose there's a reason for all the things that happened on Howey Island. I'm not sure what all those reasons are, and I'm not sure I will ever know. I do know this; fancy as the grave is, I'm the only one left to keep the thing neat and mourn the formerly wealthy dead. Mr. Howey never set foot on the island again. I will keep the weeds pulled and the leaves raked with whatever short little bit of life I have left. Not because of any love I have for Mr. Howey, but out of respect for the life he provided me and my family. What little love I have left is devoted to a small cross made of driftwood stuck in the ground next to the mausoleum. Scratched into that marker is simply "Marty and Baby Williams".

Howey James Williams was the only child of a traveling salesman and a housewife and he always knew how to make money. As a kid, he would steal fruit from the neighborhood trees. If he got caught with a "Hey kid...get outta here!" he would then pedal out to the edge of town and fill his basket from the many groves that marched off into the distance. It was a longer ride to the groves, but the fruit was low-hanging and the trees seemed to go on forever.

He would fill the basket on his bicycle to overflowing and pedal downtown. In the sweltering Florida sun, he would sell the oranges, lemons, limes, grapefruit and kumquat to the seemingly endless passersby. By the end of a good day he would have 25, or even 30 cents and a half a basket of unsold citrus that he would dump into the canal on the way home. It was no crime to waste the excess because there were plenty of trees heavy with fruit. Besides, it wasn't good business to sell day old, flyblown fruit. Fresh was what sold, so fresh was what Howey picked every single day. The coins went secretly from his bulging pocket into a cigar box under his bed. Before long, the cigar box overflowed with pennies, nickels, dimes and a few treasured quarters. The latter always acquired after grudgingly making change. Usually, Howey told the quarter patrons that he had no change, hoping they would just pay the quarter for a choice grapefruit, a pair of oranges or maybe a handful of kumquat. That only happened a few times and once and it was from a man in a dapper suit mopping his dripping brow with a handkerchief. Howey assumed, correctly, that a man who could squander an entire quarter on one piece of fruit must be a banker, a lawyer or a thief. It turns out he was two of the three, but that's a story for another time. One day, Howey took his lode of coins home and the secret box under his bed began to overflow. The next day he rode his bicycle to the shop with a big, carved wooden Indian out front. He took home in his basket five more cigar boxes from the trash out back. It didn't take too long before those were also filled with coins.

One blistering summer day, with angry thunderclouds building in the west, Howey came home from peddling his stolen wares and saw the sheriff's car in front of the little cottage he shared with his momma and his daddy. Scared that he was in trouble for nicking the fruit he sold every day, he pumped his ten-year-old legs as fast as he could away from the lawman. He hid himself deep in the groves that were the apparent source of his run-in with the law. As the sun set, and the mosquitoes rose, and his belly grumbled, and the dark sky threatened lightening, he resigned himself to his fate and slowly pedaled back home. He hoped the sheriff would be gone; off on more important crimes than his, but as he rounded the corner to his street, the black car with the star on the door was still parked there in front of his house. Even worse, the yard was filled with milling neighbors wringing their hands and talking in low whispers.

"Gee whiz", he muttered, "all this for a few nicked oranges?"
Howey rode his bike directly up the the sheriff, ready to accept his fate when he realized two people were absent from the crowd, along with his dad's old Hupmobile.

The sheriff sighed.
"Howey, I have some bad news. Your momma and your dad were hit straight on by a delivery truck that busted an axle on Route 1. They were thrown clear of the wreck and died right there on the side of the road, but not before a priest came along and offered them their last rights. The truck driver might well live, but he's for sure lost his leg"

Howey blinked at the sheriff for a few seconds, and then at the concerned faces of Mrs. Marsh and Mr. Peebles and the Nice Old Couple who lived across the street and the other faces mooning at his tragic loss. A freezing chill crept up from his balls and into his gut and finally settled

behind his eyes as they came back to rest on the sheriff.
"Thank you kindly Sheriff Grady."
His eyes were full of tears, but he wouldn't let them spill. Not
in front of this sheriff and surely not in front of his neighbors
who cared not a whit until someone died or fell ill or crippled.

The sky finally let go in great, big slow, warm
drops of lazy rain. Thunder rolled off in the not too
distant sky. The rumbles spoke of harder and faster rain,
but for now it was just a drazzle of those fat, insolent
drops. Howey got off his bicycle and let it drop on the
ground. He walked, wooden legged into the house amid
the stares and gasps and womanly weeping and went
straight to his bedroom. There he kneeled before his bed,
let his tears spill hot and salty down his cheeks and said
a prayer from rote for his mommy and daddy. When his
weeping was done he slowly pulled out six boxes full
of coins from under his bed. He carefully stacked his
cigar boxes and lugged them out the back door where no
concerned neighbors pretended to care and made his way
into the night on foot, his trusty bike already forgotten.

What happened to Howey Williams that night is
of really no concern to us. I'm sure the little boy who
eventually grew into the man that raised an empire of
citrus mourned his lost parents. I think he must have found
a place under the orange trees that started his fortune and
cried his eyes out. I like to hope that little Howey felt
sadness, and loss, and longing for mommy and daddy, but
the truth is I just don't know. That night, and the lonely
days and nights that followed are lost to the winds of time.

What we do know is that Howard James "Howey" Williams made no less than an entire fortune in citrus. He purchased hundreds of thousands of acres of cheap, sandy Florida scrub land. Did he purchase this bounty with his cigar boxes full of coins? Maybe. Likely not. He probably turned his coins into dollars and then into mortgages or deeds or whatever it is that rich men use to forge their fortunes. All we know is that upon this bedeviled land of palmettos and cockroaches and rattlesnakes, he planted enough orange, grapefruit, lemon and lime trees to make a thousand men rich. He built tin roof processing plants next to railroads and employed enough negroes to fill the passing trains with enough fruit that it might as well have been gold.

I was one of the bosses in charge of those negroes. My job was to be sure that they picked the bounty, cleaned the fruit, plucked off the stems and kept up with the loads, filling each train car to overflowing. Then on to the next. Pick, clean, pluck, fill. Over and over. Watching over them was hard, hot, sweaty, dirty work, but not nearly as hard as the work they did. Besides, it paid nearly forty dollars a week in cash and God knows, I needed the money.

To make a short story even longer, I have to tell you that I moved up in the company and got even closer and closer to Mr. Howey until I was his right-hand man. Planning rail car loads, figgering routes, hiring and firing negroes all the way up til the time they were called colored and then decided to call themselves blacks, along with country boys that could lug a hundred pound or more of fruit, all the while hating the negroes that hated them, I worked for Mr. Howey. Most days it was sun up to sundown. It was long, hard and thoughtful work, but I was grateful. I was pulling in nearly eighty dollars a week by then and it was a blessing to feed and clothe my boy and pay the rent and give my wife money for groceries, but the meals that she cooked every single day and night in the little house that Mr. Howey rented us were more delicious than any simple man could hope for. We had less than some and more than most and we were grateful.

Then one morning, Mr Howey came to the little shack by the rails that I worked out of. He said he had another job for me. I picked up my tin cup a coffee and just looked at him and nodded, yessir. I sipped the bitter coffee and I gotta tell you, my insides cramped up. I can't say I loved my job, but it was honest work and it paid good. I didn't want another one that might pay less or make me work more. He said come take a walk with me. So we walked out by the railroad tracks and he kept his head down, thoughtful, unlike I had ever seen him do before. Mr. Howey was a man who kept his head up and plowed through life like the tycoon he was. I kept my head down too and counted the railroad ties. One, two, ten, twenty, while Mr. Howey rode the thoughts drifting through his mind. Finally he looked at me and, I have to admit, I was terrified.

"I've bought an island. I want you to move to that island and be caretaker of a house that I'm building for Marty."

Now, I had only ever lived in a house. I could swing a hammer and fix a spot of plaster, but I knew nothing of caretaking a house and I told Mr. Howey that exact thing.

He snorted a bit and said I could do anything I put my mind too. Hadn't I overseen the entire operation and run the negroes and the rednecks and shipped his fruit all over the God Loving country? And I said yes, but shipping fruit is a damn sight different than overseeing a house. Especially on an island. He stopped walking and stood there on an oily railroad tie and looked at me long and hard. The bugs buzzed and the birds squawked the sweat trickled down my face and his and I looked back at him, both as long and as hard as he looked at me. Finally I broke and told Mr. Howey that if you want me to watch your house and your wife on an island, I will certainly do it. But I think a slight raise might be in order for such a task.

He looked at me cold and hard. The sweat was dripping down his face, but he was as cool as a Coca Cola in one of those electrical iceboxes that don't need no ice. Then his eyes crinkled, his mouth smiled and he laughed out loud. He told me "So we got a deal, then, son!"

I looked down at the gravel between the railroad ties under my feet and I thought about my wife. She was very pretty in a plain sort of way and she laid down to sleep with me every single night and packed my lunch bucket in the morning. Every day before the sun, I woke up and had her smell all over me and I took that smell to work with me. Sure, it faded around lunch time, but I had her cold meatloaf sandwiches and the oranges that she picked herself from the tree in the backyard and her jug of sun tea to remind me. After lunch was long picked from my teeth, I looked forward to going home to her and her sweet smell every single day. My son was a simple young man and worked in the simple way that I did, except his job was at the market, hard and honest. We didn't have much words between us, but he called my wife mom and he called me dad. There was a lot of love that went back and forth between the three of us. I thought a bit about that love and thought how hard life would be if lost it. I looked at my boss in his crinkled, amused eyes and said

"Sure thing, Mr Howey. I'll learn how to caretake of a house. Did you say on an island?"

He clapped me on the back, laughed the last laugh I ever heard him utter and told me it wasn't just any island, it was his island.

We walked back on the track to my shack and he told me all about William's Island, his paradise just off the coast, with sprawling trees that grew of their own accord and pretty sunsets and all about the big, white sunny house he was having built. For Marty. Martha Ellen, nee Sanderson, Williams. His wife that I suspect he loved dearly, although probably not quite as dearly as his empire.

I wish to this day I had run off into the buzzing, chirping woods away from Mr. Howey, and the horrors that visited us on his island and never looked back. But, I didn't and that's why I'm telling you this story before it's too late even for me.

The island is right off the coast. Maybe a mile or two from the mainland by boat. I'm here to tell you that if this island is paradise, then Hell is a free vacation with all the iced tea you can drink. It's windswept and mostly what they call scrub barrens filled with prickly weeds, stubborn palmetto, rattlesnakes and big old tortoises, likely older than me and you put together, bumbling along the hot sand

and eating the nasty weeds filled with burrs. The air swarms with wasps and hard biting flies in the daytime and clouds of blood-sucking mosquitoes in the air and cockroaches bigger than my thumb scurrying on the ground at night. Some of those cockroaches even have the nerve to fly. Dumb as they are, they fly right at you. You swat them down and lose them and then they run right at you again until you finally squish them into a crunchy mess with your foot. The starboard side was as still as death and sweltering as a hot bath in August. On the leeward side the hot wind blows steady off the water and fills your eyes with sand and gnats and the tang of salt air. On that side, just beyond a slip of sand covered in rotting sea grass that you might call a beach, there's an old graveyard. It's the only sign of human life (or rather death) you see at first. But closer to the middle of the island, there's big, tall pines and cypress and a huge and ancient banyan tree. A sandy path leads to the middle and it's a hard to road to walk on; a truck full of supplies would surely get stuck there. The soft, hot, sugary sand steals a step for every one or two you take. Unless you oiled that road down, which is exactly the first thing Mr. Howey did. If you ever walked an oiled sand road in July, then you know exactly what the road to Hell feels like. Long about the end of the road that got oiled was the house Mr. Howey had almost finished building. It was white clapboard, two stories and an attic tall, built smack next to that huge old banyan tree. Banyon trees don't exactly grow out of the ground like other trees. Their seeds nestle in the crevices of other trees and they grow until they eventually strangle their host. They throw out vinelike roots directly from their big, sprawling branches to the ground that grow into thick, woody trunks that become as big as goodly sized trees themselves. The result is a confusing mess of roots, vines and huge shading canopy that casts a gigantic shadow and looks like a small forest. I swear it looked like the tree owned that house. Even though that house was not done being built, it squatted next to that banyan tree and looked as if it had been there a hundred years or more. The house looked nice enough by itself, but next to that tree it just looked wrong. Level and plumb and well-nailed it was. Mr. Howey never spared no expense, but that house looked all slanted and, well, just off. But, I'm getting ahead of myself. I'd be better to just tell it as it happened.

Mr. Howey took me to the island a few weeks after our walk down the rail tracks. We went in a little skiff that smelled like dead fish with a colored boy tilling the smoky, noisy engine in the back. It was choppy and hot out and the little skiff bounded over each wave like an idiot dog chasing a ball down a hill. Now, I've lived near the ocean my whole life, and stepped into it to fish and even swim on occasion, but I was never much for riding up on it. Before long, and I mean about two minutes, I was green to the gills and felt like dying or puking my guts out. Mr. Howey stood at the bow with a lit cigar like a general in some old painting and pointed out this and that on the island all the while puffing out clouds of smoke that made me think puking and dying might just be a blessing. I nodded and grunted and tried to keep my eyes glued to the deck, to the rail, to the colored boy in the back, to anything but the horizon that bobbed up and down and tried to keep the wind in my lungs instead of the rancid cigar smoke puffing from Mr. Howey.

Finally, mercifully, the skiff crunched up onto the shelly beach. Mr. Howey stepped off like he was Christopher Columbus discovering the New World, not even getting a drop of water on his expensive brown loafers. I stumbled out the boat, plopped my right foot into the water and nearly fell flat on my face, coughing and trying not to puke. Mr. Howey grabbed my arm and grunted "Steady Boy" and with a tight push, nearly threw me into the sand. I gained my footing, and a small bit of my self respect, and stood looking at the desolation that was Howey Island.

Howey looked back at the colored boy, told him to pull the boat up, throw out the anchor and mind the tide and then launched into a narrative of the island:

"This island was a fishing village back in the 1800's. It started out as a camp for fishermen that didn't want to head all the way inland when they knew they had to fish early the next morning. They would head in at dusk, beach their little boats, salt their catch and stoke a fire. Around the fire they would pass a bottle of whiskey, roll cigarettes and smoke and tell the tales fishermen tell. When they got tired, they would sleep by the fire. When the sun rose, they would wake up, boil bitter coffee on the embers, drink a bit more whiskey and head back out to get their fill of fish and crabs and shrimp. Only when their fish boxes were full would they make their way to the mainland and sell their catch. This went on a for a good bit until some enterprising fisherman built a tent against the ugly Florida sun and rain and mosquitoes. Other fisherman pitched their own tents and talked their talk and drank their whiskey and coffee. Then one day, a fisherman skipped taking his catch for a few days and brought over some rough lumber and tar in his boat and built a shanty. The shanty grew over time to a shack and then to nearly a real house. Other fisherman got the idea and took days off from their catch to nearly build

their own houses and shanties. Soon it made sense for the fisherman to just stay on the island, go out every day and fish and then take their catch to the mainland when they were full up or needed salt to keep the fish or tar to patch their roofs. This went for a quite a bit more and eventually the men grudgingly brought their lonely women and babies over and made a right community of the whole mess. As we all know, a community of living people includes people that die sooner or later and at first they buried their dead with a only cross of driftwood, or building lumber, to mark the spot. This was fine for a bit, but the same fisherman who built the first shanty, now old and knocking on the door that we never walk back through, thought that maybe driftwood markers just weren't the right way to honor the dead. The old fisherman took his last trip to the mainland and with his last pocketful of cash money and commissioned a stonemason to make a small grave marker with his own damned name on it. He plowed back through waves, his little boat laden with a heavy stone and died three days later. The residents of the unnamed island dug him a proper grave, wrapped his body in oyster sacks and laid him to rest. At the head of this first proper grave that the island accepted, they propped up his small headstone. To this day, it's one of the few headstones still standing. Life on the island went along for quite a few years as a rough village of rough and scrappy men and their few women and even fewer grubby children. There were few friends, fewer acquaintances and mostly strangers eking out a living and competing with each other to catch and sell their sea food. When a boat failed to return from the sea for a week or more, a man would pass around a hat, gather up what bit of money he could and head to the mainland. There he would find the stonemason and commission a headstone that simply read "Captain". He would lug this headstone back on his boat (it was small but heavy) and the islanders would say a prayer and stick the headstone in the ground. They would then go about their business knowing full well that tomorrow any one of them might earn a headstone with the same words and an empty grave. No one on that island could truthfully say it was a good life, but it was life, and they ate and slept and bred and it was the only life they knew how to live. Sometimes, a man or a woman or both would fall sick and die and a fisherman would skip his days catch and haul over to the mainland with a pocketful of money to buy a headstone. Sometimes they knew a name to etch on the stone, mostly they didn't and couldn't spell it if they did. This is how, over the years, the cemetery on the unnamed island, later known as Howey's, grew. Then one morning, the fishermen, their wives and children woke up to see the sun rising in the east and a black horizon in the west. The men knew a bad storm when they saw one, but also knew they had to get their fill of fish. They stood around, smoking and sipping whiskey for a bit and decided that they could fish the morning, be back early and head inland or even to mainland by afternoon before the storm hit. The women looked worried and some even begged for the men to not go, but this was a time when men were men and the fish didn't catch themselves. So, the men headed out towards the black sky. The hurricane was closer and faster than the men figured and not a one of them was ever found, not even a sliver of a piece of a boat. The hurricane barreled up on the island and turned the surf into an angry froth. The women, peering out at the sea all morning under hands that looked like salutes, saw the coming fury in the waves. When the wind picked up to a howl, they gathered up the children, some supplies and headed into the snake infested, tangled scrubland of the island interior. They were right, in some small measure, to head inland of the island, but there was never really any hope for them. When the full fury of the storm hit, it lashed the island with winds the like of which no human there had ever witnessed. The trees bent over almost to the ground and whipped back, the sand flew in whirling dervishes that blinded and lacerated the huddling women and crying children. They huddled under the branches and between the weird vertical roots of an ancient banyan tree that seemed so old that God himself planted the thing. If the storm had just been the vicious wind, they may have survived, but the relentless wind pushed a wall of water eighteen feet tall before it. One old woman chose to stay behind to stand on the beach and taunt the storm. She shook her veiny fist at the onslaught and screeched "Is that all you got? Fuck You!" When she first saw the wall of water more than a mile out, her knees grew a bit weak, but she stood her ground, certain that the wave would break in the shallow waters offshore, Her fist dropped and her "Fuck You" turned to "Dear God" when she watched the wave not even hesitate over the shallows. As she stood there, watching a wall of water barreling forward tall over her head, "Dear God" turned into "Hail Mary full of gr" and she was swept towards the center of the island at better than one hundred and fifty miles per hour. Mercifully, her head was dashed on a piece of hard ground and she never even knew she drowned. The women and children cowering under the banyan tree were not so lucky. The unrelenting surge of ocean water, containing the fish that made their living and the crabs and shrimp and a few sharks and even a panicked porpoise, hit them like the end of the world. Which it certainly was for those unfortunate souls. Some were carried away, some were pounded against the banyan roots, some were trapped by the shelter they thought would keep them safe and drank deeply into their lungs the dark, roiled water. The storm bashed on for hours and swirled the bodies of the dead around the roots of the banyan until it was spent and the water that ended an island life for so many finally decided it was done and went back to where it belonged. The next morning, sunny and bright and full of hope, a few relatives boated over the the island in the hopes of finding survivors. Their hopes were in vain because when they saw what the storm left behind, some men gasped, some puked and most all prayed aloud. Tangled in the complicated roots of the banyan tree were the twisted and broken bodies and parts of bodies of the women and children that weren't swept out to sea. They tended, as best they could, to the broken bodies and arms and legs and even a head wedged between a thick root that they found. They laid the remains out and did their best to identify who was what, but in the end they named one woman by her arm. On the gnarled, gripping hand was a ring that was known because it was bought by a proud fisherman to tempt this once vital young woman to be his wife. That arm earned a grave marker that read "Captain Bill and His Wife". The stonemason boated over with a load of blank granite headstones and helped bury the few, broken pathetic dead that were left. He chiseled granite until his hands bled and his knuckles swelled with missed mallet strikes until he fell over; starved and thirsty because there was no food to eat nor water to drink on this island of death. He boated back after his labors with empty pockets, empty belly and an empty soul. He lasted one drunken day on the mainland before he woke up from his stupor the next morning before dawn to realize that his heart had stopped. He did the only thing he could and fell *over and died. He was laid to rest on the mainland under a stone his apprentice carved in his honor. His name was well known, and well carved into his stone. It was the last thing his apprentice carved before he walked away from the stoneyard and was never seen again. From that time forward five years, there were no headstones to be had for fifty miles. In the end good folks abandoned all the island had to offer. And there it sat, untended and forgotten until...*

"I bought it for a song. That lawyer and his crazy ideas of lineage this and history that. I paid the judge a few bucks and a case of whatever that lush drinks, and here we are! The latest addition to the Williams Empire!"

I swatted away some angry buzzing thing and absently nodded to Mr. Howey. He frowned and waved for me to follow him. I wasn't sure that I heard what I thought I just heard. I chalked it up to the rough boat ride and the thick cigar smoke. Despite the heat radiating off the sand, a chill ran down my spine.

We walked up the oiled road with the sad, forgotten cemetery to our right, the hot ocean breeze at our backs and nothing but scrub and brush everywhere else rustling with God knows what.

Mr. Howey droned on about the various plants and trees that grew here all by themselves. All I saw were ugly weeds and stunted brown things that looked like they wanted to be trees, but just gave up. It seemed to me that the good folks didn't abandon this island. It was more like the island took everything they had to give and what was left was buried near where that shitty little boat landed. But, who am I to judge? I followed along as the road curved slightly to the north and I finally saw a structure in the near distance.

"Is that your house, Mr. Howey?"

He looked at me like I was an idiot and I instantly realized my mistake. As we got closer I could see that it was way too small to be a house, even though it had columns and a facade. It was indeed a small house, maybe almost bigger than mine, but it was huge for a death house. Mr. Howey explained that this was where he would be buried. Or laid out. Or whatever it is they do with a dead body in, what he explained, was a mausoleum. Mr. Howey informed me that a man who is important in life, must also be important in death. I didn't understand that at all, but I just nodded like I knew all about important dead folks. We walked past the mausoleum and I saw the whole thing looked to be made out of gravestone material: marble. Howard James Williams was carved into the stone right above a wrought iron door that stood half open and had fancy colored windows. Why the dead needed windows was beyond me, but I kept my mouth shut and just looked and walked.

While I was walking and staring in awe at the place where Mr. Howey would rot, I didn't notice that the house for living people was now within sight. When my gaze first settled on that house, I felt like I did in the stench of the cigar fouled fish boat. There was a brief moment when I thought I would just pass out right there on the oily sand road. Mr. Howey didn't even notice because he was beaming ear-to-ear with his arms outswept proclaiming "Welcome to Williams Island Manor!" I walked past Mr. Howey's proud arms and looked at the house. My head felt like it was filled with the flies buzzing around in the stifling late morning air. I stood there and looked at it. My mind kept saying look away now. Don't cast another eye upon the thing, but something else kept saying look at it, just look at it. I did a little of both and looked away from it and at it. Nothing could change the fact that this house simply looked wrong. The angles were off, there wasn't a level part of it, but as I glanced away, and then back it looked sorta right again. Next to the house stood an enormous banyan tree that looked like it had been here since the dawn of time. It rose nearly forty feet in the air and was a tangled puzzle of massive crawling roots and immense reaching branches. The lower branches had ropey vines tickling the ground and thick, trunk-like roots that seemed to reach up from the ground to connect with the branches. It was hard to tell if the tree was growing out of the ground, or into it. I felt confused and hot and woozy and more than a bit tired of all this bullshit. But, my boss was standing beside me with an idiot look of pride for what he bought and built. The man paid my weekly check so I bucked up and followed his outstretched arm to the wooden, unpainted front steps.

As I walked up the steps I could smell the piney smell of fresh cut wood. Under that was the sharp smell of cedar and under that, another smell. Of course. If you build a house on a wet island full of bugs, you'll want to use cedar. It's a pungent and hard wood. Bugs don't eat cedar. But bugs eat dead things and that was the smell that lay over everything like a wet blanket forgotten in the basement of an abandoned insane asylum. I walked through the front doorway, which didn't yet have a door attached to it, and stepped from the dazzling sunlight and into a dream which quickly became a nightmare.

The smell of fresh cut cedar and pine was instantly replaced with the rich smell of ocean water and fish and shellfish and the long since rotted dead. I heard the distraught screams of women yelling where are the children. I heard the howl of the wind and a crash as a tree was snapped from its roots and hurled by the wind, cutting off human limbs and killing the lucky ones who would have drowned. I smelled blood and death and worse. I slowly turned and looked out the the big window and saw a banyan root that I knew cut a little five year old girl in half, dashed by the relentless tide and a mother screamed, her voice gargled by saltwater and the bodies flowed, the screams competed with the howling wind and Mr Howey asked me "How do you like it? Are you ok, boy? You look a little peaked. Here's the kitchen with all the best new electric and gas appliances" I followed Mr. Howey into the kitchen where an old lady lay broken; her head held on by a thread of flesh on her throat who silently screamed to me "Get out. Now. While you still can!" And the rushing water washed most of her away too. Except her head, which had caught in the knee root of the tree. The tide swirled and her body snapped free of her head. She silently mouthed her unheeded warning as her skinny, wrinkled naked body went out with the tide.

I mopped my sweaty face with a shaky hand and told my boss, that yes indeedy, this was a mighty fine kitchen. A woman could certainly serve a delicious meal from here. Meat and mashed potatoes and vegetables and cakes could well be made here. And breakfast! Oh my, yes! Bacon and eggs and biscuits and gravy, oh YES! Gosh, I'm getting hungry just THINKING about it.

Mr   Howey gave me an odd look, but he was so wrapped up in the   El Grande tour of his freshly built abode that he simply guided me by the elbow back out into the main hall towards the freshly painted cedar staircase leading upstairs. I knew it was freshly painted because the tang of turpentine settled in the back of my throat along with the now familiar smell of cedar and and dank ocean water and rotting flesh.

I said ,

" Shouldn't we see the rest of the first floor first, Sir?"

Mr Howey psshd and informed me that the best part was the upstairs sitting room.

"You just HAVE to SEE it"

I looked in Mr. Howey's eyes and was not even mildly assured that this was a room I just HAD to SEE. I saw the reflection of the stairs in Mr. Howey's sweaty bald head and I just wanted to piss my pants or run right the hell out of there, or both. I managed to command myself to swallow the sawdust that was in my throat with a loud click and just smiled a lunatic's smile and nodded.

All I knew at that moment was that a brace of wild horses could not drag me up those stairs, yet one leaden foot clomped on the first stair, and feet being the inseparable pair that they are, the other one followed. Inside my head a lunatic thought capered and screamed "Don't Go Don't GoDontgoDONTGODONTGO. One idiot foot followed the other up the steps, my nose nearly level to Mr. Howey's perfumed, yet smelly ass and up the stairs I went. When I reached the landing, I looked down at the world I wished I was still part of and then around at the doors leading off into the various rooms and water closets that lead off in all directions. The idiot in my head screamed "HOW MANY ROOMS ARE THERE??? WE'LL NEVER GET OUT" I told my inner idiot to shut the fuck up, this is work, you moron, and looked around.

I was presented with a clean, well built space. Wainscotting crawled halfway up the wall and wallpaper filled in the rest of the way, it was a nice, open upper landing with a solid oaken floor underfoot. Hmph. I thought. Stop acting like a shrinking flower. We perused the guest rooms (four) and then the bathrooms; two. One with a tub, one with only a commode and a gleaming white porcelain sink. I started feeling better. Not so queasy and not quite as sweaty. Then we went into the master bedroom with its wide windows looking through the banyan branches out onto the front yard. When I saw the half of a little boy crawling across the floor dragging his intestines behind him, I didn't shit my pants, but I did feel a squirt of warm piss run down my leg. He didn't cry, he just gestured behind himself and asked "Hey Mister, couldja help me find the rest of my gullet? I reckon I can get by without my legs, but I think I may need the rest of my guts" I laughed a bit and threw up in my mouth a bit and swallowed it back down and, well yea, pissed down my leg a little bit more. Mr. Howey was busy showing me where the bed would be; facing the window, of course, and that idiot laugh burbled out some and when I followed his hands where the dresser would be placed is when I noticed the little girl. She was cute and unharmed, but soaked to the skin. She smiled at me and that smile melted my heart. She was mouthing something, but I couldn't hear what she was saying, so I moved a bit closer, my head cocked to the side. When I moved closer, I noticed she had something in her hand that she kep trying to put around her shoulder. It was too heavy for her so I reached down to try to help her. I saw that she was about eight and had dark hair and big brown eyes. She smiled at me and that smile seemed to slough off the obvious hallucinations I was experiencing. I shucked up my cuffs and kneeled down next to her to help with whatever she was trying to lift. I gave her my best smile and reached out for what she was struggling with. She handed me her mom's arm and pointed to a torso bobbing in the swirling water. Even in my horror, I reached for the arm, but it and the girl and the torso were swept away in a vicious wave and I was left there squatting on my haunches hearing the gurgling scream of a little girls lungs fill with water. As the frothy water grabbed the arm, I saw that it had a ring on one finger.

I had already pissed myself so shitting myself wouldn't be that much of a stretch, but somehow I managed to clamp my asshole shut, vaguely wondering if any of the fancy bathrooms had running water (HAHA RUNNING WATER MAY VERY WELL BE THE PROBLEM HERE) yet.

I stood up after pretending to admire the wooden flooring and Mr. Howey proclaimed "Ready to see the best room of all? The Nursery! Yes, that's right, my good man! Marty's gonna have a little Howey!"

I screamed at Mr. Howey, "Are you crazy? This place is floating with rotted dead bodies and disembodied children and you WANT TO PUT YOUR WIFE AND A BABY HERE ARE YOU

NUTS?" in my mind, and said aloud "Sure thing, sir"

We walked through a door that I hadn't noticed before into a room right off the master suite. It was cheery and already painted baby blue. Hmm..optimistic, I thought. What if its a girl? Then I saw the bay window leaning crazily out right into the banyan branches. I heard the snap of a twig and outside the window a broken doll floated by in a rushing, frothy wave. I leaned closer to the window and saw that it was a broken baby, mouth still open in a silent bawl.

Right then I knew what I had to do. I told Mr. Howey "Great house. Nice baby blue nursery. I'm sure Mrs. Williams will love it, but don't you think maybe you should let her give birth on the mainland? Doctors, hospitals, medicine and the lack of (dead people floating by) disease and infection?"

I raised my eyebrows in their most earnest position and waited to either get fired or to hear the voice of reason. I got neither when my boss exclaimed "Nonsense, boy. I built this house for my family and this is where my family will be raised"

I nodded my best
"Youknowbestsirofcourseyessiree"
and followed him down the stairs with only one backward glance. I was hoping at least the little girl that gave me her mom's arm made it out ok, but I only saw a neat and tidy landing.

We perused the parlor and the library and I only saw one woman get savaged by a shark that was longer than the boat that brought us here. This was somehow worse than everything else because she was alive the entire time it ate her. First a leg was ripped off. It played with her, bumping her against a root or a rock, then it dashed in to take the other leg. She lolled there, blood turning the water a bubbling, frothy red. She looked at me pleading, but what could I do? I watched hopelessly as the shark circled and swallowed her right arm almost all the way to the shoulder. It clamped down on its meal with its thousand teeth and shook its head back and forth; whipsawing the limb off leaving trails of ragged flesh. She only grimaced and stared at me with an accusation that I refused to accept. It came back and grabbed her left arm and part of her shoulder, she looked at the shark and it appeared they were so eye to eye that they were sharing some intimate secret, but then the shark ripped off the limb and its attachment and she mouthed a silent scream as blood squirted into the air. I wondered how her heart could still pump so much blood and I shoved my fist in my mouth to stifle my own scream, sure that that carnage was over. But no, apparently the shark was not done gorging on the poor woman. Time ticked by like a broken clock and the blood flow slowed, yet the shark came back and consumed the rest of her torso all the way to nearly the top of her lungs. I know this because after the shark bit, shook and swam off with his tidbit, I could see the bits of lung and entrails drifting in the swirling water. She couldn't scream anymore, but she was alive, oh yes, as it bit down and slashed its head back and forth tearing the last bit of her apart. She was well aware as it ate every bit of her except her head with the wildly staring eyes which looked directly into mine and her mouth silently spoke words I never want to hear. The roiling water tossed her mangled remains against the roots of the banyan tree and finally, mercifully, she went under the water and didn't surface.

We walked back out onto the front steps and the sunlight was like little daggers stabbing my eyes. Without knowing it, I mimicked the women of ages ago shielding their eyes from the coming horror of the hurricane; an absent salute. Mr. Howey asked if I thought I could caretake of his new house and I nodded once, not knowing what else I could possibly say. How could I speak of the torn children and women that I had seen ravaged by sea and surf and sharks? Because I did see them. I know I did. The only other option was that I had gone stark, raving mad in one afternoon. I didn't feel good, but I didn't feel insane either. I still wonder to this day if maybe I am insane and not aware of it. Insane would be a blessing; insane would wrap around me like a warm blanket on a cold Saturday night or a cool sheet on a warm Sunday morning. Anything but this would be a comfort. But, I decided then that I was not mad, that I saw what I saw and Mrs. Howey must never set foot on this cursed place, especially not ripe with child. I walked with Mr. Howey on rubbery legs to the anchored skiff while storm clouds built in the west and sent the waters all the way back across the bay to the mainland upset and angry. The skiff slapped and slammed on the heavy waves while I stared ahead and Mr. Howey smoked his cigar.

The main house was mostly finished by the end of the next month and I was installed there in a special caretakers house that was a surprise for me from Mr. Howey. It was built well away from the banyan tree, so thankfully, I didn't see any bodies floating by and didn't witness any horrific dismemberments. It was a nice little cottage. White clapboard to match the big house, but only one story, one bedroom and one bathroom. It had a nice kitchen with an oven and a sink and hot and cold running water. The two nights I slept there I couldn't even hear the screams of the nearly dead or the howl of the winds. It was quite peaceful.

My wife was, of course, distraught to hear that I would be gone for a month, back home for a day or two, and gone again. But, I explained this meant a big raise that would help us in our future. She argued that what kind of future could we have if we don't live for today and love each other right now? She begged to come to the island and stay with me since our boy was growing and could tend to himself, and I told her that she was to never set foot on that island as long as she lived. I didn't raise my voice, but the seriousness and finality of my tone came through loud and clear. She looked at me; hurt and sad and turned away to go to bed. I slept on the couch that night for the first time ever. The next morning we had few words. I told her I loved her and she said she loved me too, but there was a gulf between us bigger than the choppy water I had to cross to reach the hell that was Howey's Island.

As the skiff plowed through that choppy water, delivering me to my first day as caretaker of the island, I wasn't as queasy as I was on the first ride. There was a warm breeze and the sky was a clear, smooth blue above; and of course, no cigar stench because Mr. Howey had no need to be there. I was alone on the skiff with just my ditty bag and the colored boy. The solitude gave me a chance to admire the island. It was a swath of dark green perched atop the emerald water. It was really quite a beautiful place. From a distance, anyway. As it grew steadily closer, I could see the gnarled trees and scrub and towering above it all, the mighty banyan tree in the middle of the island.

As we approached the beach, the smell of dead fish filled my nostrils. In the water were hundreds, if not thousands of dead fish. I turned to the colored boy and asked why the fish died, and he just cupped his ear and shook his head. He couldn't hear me over the drone of the outboard. When we landed on the beach, dead fish lapping up with the small wave pushed by the bow, I grabbed my ditty and jumped off into the sand. Not a drop of water splashed on my workboots. I turned to my driver, grinning proudly at my newfound sea legs. I expected him to cut the engine so I could ask again about the dead fish and perhaps offer him a small tip for his effort, but he was already pushing the boat back out with an old wooden oar. He waved, turned the tiller hard and my smelly little connection to the mainland burbled away, running from it's wake and belching blue exhaust. The driver never even gave me a backward glance.

I stood there on the seaweed covered beachlet and listened as the droning sound of the boat's engine gave way to the gentle lapping sound of the water. A lone seagull seemed to laugh as it circled above and a cricket chirped in the grass, apparently mistaking day for night. I glanced over at the cemetery and it just looked forlorn and unkempt. It was hot, but not nearly as stifling as it was when I visited with Mr. Howey. I thought back about his story of the island and the hurricane and all the death and decided that I must have imagined the whole thing. I felt a painful twinge of regret for not allowing my wife to come with me. What the hell was wrong with me? Lightheaded from a boat ride and cigar smoke and I act like a total idiot. I resolved that when my choppy ride came back next month to collect me I would invite her to come along. Or maybe I could catch a ride back sooner with one of the workers finishing up the house. Surely there were men going back and forth from the island to the mainland every day. With this pleasant thought in my mind, I picked up my ditty bag and marched up the oiled road with a light step and an even lighter heart.

I passed the mausoleum and noticed that the wrought iron door was closed and locked tight. I briefly wondered why someone would lock an empty grave. I mentally shrugged and carried on. When I rounded the curve and spied the big house in the cool, green shade of the tree, the thin sheen of sweat on my brow chilled a bit. It felt good to have the sun off my face. Nothing seemed off about the house at all. I chuckled a bit at my former hallucination, dropped my bag on the ground and stopped to admire the scene; hands on my hips. It was a beautifully crafted, rambling, white clapboard house. The roofs peaked up almost three stories into the shade of the big tree which was so close to the house that it seemed as if it was hugging it protectively. About three hundred yard from the big house sat my little cottage. Gleaming white and shaded by a copse of cypress trees. I approved mightily of the scene and reached down to pick up my bag. when I stood back up and headed towards the cottage, I glanced one more time at the big house and the lines and angles looked all wrong once again. The tree was crouching over it like a hungry spider with its fangs sucking the very reality of the house. I blinked and it was just a big house with a big tree next to it. I cajoled myself to stop falling victim to my fruitful imagination and walked on. About halfway to the cottage, I realized that I should ask a worker about that ride back to the mainland. Maybe I could catch a ride later today and surprise the wife. After all, Mrs. Howey was not due to land here for another three days. I turned on my heel and trudged towards the big house, set my ditty bag on the first step and walked up the steps to the newly installed front door. It was a handsome piece of workmanship, painted gleaming white and inset with the same colored glass as the mausoleum, which seemed a bit macabre, but I figgered they had some glass left over so why not use it?

I knocked on the door and waited a few seconds before I realized that you don't have to knock on a door attached to a house in which no one lives. I grasped the big brass lever and pushed the door open loudly proclaiming
"Hello? Anyone here?"
My greeting was met with utter silence. I heard no sounds of men hard at work with saws, nor hammers pounding. Not even the swish of a wet paintbrush caressing wooden trim. "Hello?"
The house was as quiet and still as a dormouse. Dust motes floated lazily through the air, illuminated by the sun streaming through the big windows. I walked the lower floor, hoping to find a worker snoozing the morning away, perhaps on a kitchen countertop or in a coat closet, but the first level was devoid of a single soul save my own. The furniture, recently delivered, crouched under white drop cloths like children pretending to be ghosts on All Hallow's Eve. I warily gazed up the stairs to the second level, remembering the spell I had last I was there and admonished myself again for acting like a little girl. I took the stairs two at a time, shouting out to any worker who might not have heard me. The last thing I wanted was to surprise a carpenter and get whacked on the head by a stout hammer. When I reached the landing, I walked quickly and glanced in all the doors, I realized I was truly alone. The house was finished, the workers gone and the place was

all mine. At least, for the next three days. Beads of sweat had popped out on my forehead and I swiped absently with my forearm, disappointed that I probably could not get an early boat ride back and wouldn't see my sweet wife until the months end.

As I turned in the landing to head down the stairs I heard a little voice behind me say: "Please mister, can you help me find my gut? I keep eating, but I'm still hungry" My feet denied my forward motion when I heard that voice. I looked over my shoulder and saw the young boy, maybe five years old, the lower half of his body gone. He was munching on a gobbet of flesh attached to a bone that looked like the calf of a human leg. He chewed a piece off, swallowed it and I saw the chunk of meat squirt out where his belly should have been. I'm pretty sure I screamed as I tumbled ass over teakettle down the stairs and everything went as blank as a radio being switched off.

I came to some time later with a throbbing headache and a painfully twisted knee on the first floor of the house. The sun had long since dropped below the horizon, but being summer, there was still a colorful orange and red light in the sky. This little bit of hope in the form of waning sunshine got my gimpy ass to at least try to sit up.

While I finally mustered the will to sit up, I felt a painful throbbing in my head. I tried to stand and felt my left leg scream in agony. I stopped with a wide grimace cemented to my face and breathed heavily through my teeth until the wave of agony, nausea and confusion passed. Still, I soldiered on and somehow got myself upright through the fog of pain. Using the wall as a brace, I hobbled down the hall and out of the big house through the fancy front door and onto the expansive porch. I looked at the stairs leading down to the ground and thought theres no way I can make it that far. I stopped for a moment, leaning against the white boards that made this house so pretty and bright. I took a deep breath, full of turpentine and woodsy smell and resolved myself to walk down those stairs even if it took one foot at a time. Which is exactly how it went; one good foot on a stair, one hand gripping the rail, one bum foot painfully follows, one good foot, one good hand, one bad foot. On and on it went until I finally made it to the bottom and plopped down on the last step, sweaty and spent from my efforts and wondered, not for the last time, what the hell I was doing here and what the hell was wrong with me. My ditty bag was still there curled up on the bottom step like an obedient dog and I thought maybe it could wait til tomorrow. I could barely carry my own self. Carrying my bag full of dungarees and shirts and underwear was beyond my ability at the moment. What I needed now was a cane or a walking stick to help me get to the cottage.

I glanced around and saw what I needed in a small pile of lumber left behind by the workmen. I hobbled over to the wood pile and picked out a stout board that fit just under my armpit. As I braced myself on the board, I felt a bit better to be at least physically stable, but still bothered by my fall and the utterly unstable reason for tumbling down the stairs. I had seen the forlorn little boy twice now. What could it mean other than I was losing my mind? I refused to accept that he was real. It was more comforting to think I had gone insane. That must be it; my mind had snapped like a worn out belt attached to a crazily spinning flywheel. It must be the pressure of my new job as caretaker. So much to worry over: food, (the tides) supplies, a very pregnant Mrs. Howey, (the tides and the moon) and meeting the supply boats and (the gathering storm, black on the horizon) and all the other many and sundry tasks I was now responsible for scheduling, overseeing and completing. The relentless, pounding tide splashing gently on the little beach and washing through my mind salty tasting and fishy smelling only made my tasks that much more seemingly impossible.

When I woke up the the sun was on the other side of the island. My head felt full of coarse sand made of crushed seashells. My arms and neck and legs were covered with itching welts. I laid there a few moments, trying to see through the pounding fog of pain and listening to the whine of the mosquitoes sucking my blood. I swatted at a few and was rewarded with a spatter of my own blood squirted from their engorged little bodies. I sat up slowly, like a man nursing a particularly bad hangover, which I suppose, is exactly what I had: A hangover from a stupid illusion and an even stupider tumble down some stairs. I tried to swing my legs off the couch and onto the floor and was rewarded with an excruciating pain that bolted up through my knee and into my head, both pounding in concert with my heart. I had a bad moment of dizziness, with sparkly lights in the corners of my eyes, where I thought I might pass out, but I took a deep breath, held it and slowly let it out. The dizziness passed, but my head still throbbed. I looked around and realized that I had somehow made it to the cottage. The thought of a well-stocked cupboard full of coffee and food, and perhaps aspirin, got me moving. My half-assed crutch was lying on the floor beside the couch so I picked it, and myself up, and hobbled into the little kitchen.

Which was well-stocked indeed with not simply food and coffee, but sugar, flour, iced fish and salted red meat by the pounds. I was certain that I had never seen this much uncooked food stocked up in one place in my entire life. The cupboards were full to overflowing with dry goods and there was even an electric icebox filled to the brim with frozen meats and fish and shrimp and crabs with big pointy claws. There was a part of the electric icebox, that didn't freeze, full of bottled beers, sodas and bottles of fresh milk and orange juice. I thought that if my wife saw this much food and drink in one place, she would surely faint. I grabbed a cold beer, which would make her give me that look, and resolved to find a way to get her over here. If for no other reason than to see so much food stocked in such a little place. I grasped the cold beer realizing that I had left my pocketknife in my bag back on the steps of the big house and had no way to open it. My thoughts drifted back to the things I thought I saw at the big house. I shook my head as if to convince myself that none of it was true. As I stood there in the kitchen of my new home and pondered whether I was mad or not, I noticed a bottle opener that was thoughtfully nailed to the wall right next to the icebox. I propped the lid of my beer bottle into the opening and popped the lid off with a satisfying hisss. The beer went down smooth and cold and I only had a brief moment wondering why a grown, working man would be drinking beer at this early hour of the morning. I pushed the thought away because surely no one would ever know. Besides, it tasted so good. I took another swig, set the bottle on the small counter and rummaged in the icebox for some bacon and eggs.

After a few minutes of looting through the drawers

and cabinets, I found a pan and a plate and a spatula and a fork. I commenced to frying up a healthy, man's breakfast and then sat at the small, round table and gobbled the whole mess, mopping it up with bread and washing it down with the rest of my beer. I belched, and then farted and thought maybe another cold beer might just be the right idea. I hobbled over to the icebox, grabbed another cold bottle, snapped the lid off and drank down half of the amber liquid.

I reached into my shirt pocket and pulled out a pack of Camels. I shook one out, lit it with a match and blew a cloud of blue smoke up to the ceiling. As I sat there smoking, I thought about the big house and my tumble down the stairs. Foolishness, all of it. I was ashamed of having what was obviously a fainting spell; and a tad bit worried. Maybe I should see Doc Miller when I got back home and get some kind of medicine. Ha, the Doc takes a bit much of his own medicine and it comes in a bottle with a cork. I stubbed my smoke out on my plate and tested my bum knee. I stood up with just the table for support and felt the twang of pain in my knee like a fiddle string tuned up too tight. I reached over and grabbed my half-assed crutch and wandered through the cottage, checking the place out. It didn't take long: the place was all of three rooms. A main room which consisted of the living room and kitchen with a couch, a high back chair, and a small, round dinner table with two wooden chairs, the icebox and a sink and the stocked cupboards. There was a small bedroom with a single bed and wooden dresser (have to get another one of those for the missus) and a small bathroom with a tub, a sink with a mirror over it and pull-chain commode. Oh, and electric lights on the ceiling with built-in push-button switches. Mr. Howey certainly spared no expense. There was also some oil lanterns mounted up on the wall in each room, to supply light when the power went down. Which I'm sure it did out here quite often, (when the clouds gather black on the horizon and the wind screams across the bay) especially in the summer. I wondered how Mr. Howey even got the electricity to the island. It had to be through cables from the mainland, unless there was a power plant somewhere on the island. Electricity was a dangerous mystery to me, but I resolved to find out how it was supplied to the island in case I had to switch it on if it went off, which electricity is well known to do. Mr. Howey had left me with a handwritten list of things to do here and the instructions for the electricity would surely be in there. Being a caretaker means you take care of everything. With that thought in mind, I limped out of the cottage, into the morning sunshine and set off back to the big house, my board planted firmly in my armpit.

It was already hot out for this early in the morning and somewhat slow going. Sweat trickled down into my ass crack and quickly soaked my shirt. My knee still hurt like a kicked mongrel, but my belly was full with a solid breakfast and two beers, so I switched my crutch to a cane and that seemed to speed things up and work my bum knee a bit. I stopped about halfway to the big house and surveyed my surroundings. The big house was indeed big. The banyan tree was even bigger, towering over the house and throwing cool shade. I could see now why he picked this spot to build his mansion; the way the tree spread its (arms) branches over the house, it would keep it cool all the day long. Why one man and his wife and child would need such a big house was beyond me. I glanced back at the cottage and thought if it had just one more room, it would be more than plenty for three. I shrugged, not pretending to understand how a rich man spends his money and continued on towards the big house.

I walked up to the front steps and noticed my bag sitting there, still damp from the dew. I hoped it wasn't full of spiders or cockroaches or worse, but there was nothing I could do about it at the moment so I left it sit there. I took a closer look at the banyan tree and was amazed at the size of the roots and the complicated vines. It seemed to me that it was too close to the house, but I'm not a builder and maybe that was on purpose to throw as much shade as possible. I saw a green lizard crawling on the huge trunk-like vines that were connected to the ground and a black trundle-beetle struggling up a root. The lizard eyed the beetle and in a flash, it scurried down and pounced on the beetle. The lizard ate the beetle alive in chomping bites and scurried back up the tree to its vine. It cocked its head towards me, looked me in the eye, did a few push-ups and seemed to say "Bugger off, mate. This is my vine." I chuckled and told the lizard, "Sure thing, buddy. You can have the whole damned tree".

The lizard seemed satisfied with his triumph and scurried up even higher; a scaly victor in his little domain. I looked closer at the roots of the tree and saw (a boy's leg ripped off at the hip a leather shoe still attached to the foot) many more lizards and beetles and ants crawling to and fro. One particularly large root had more beetles than the others along with more lizards stalking them. I leaned a bit closer and saw that the beetles were (eating a human hand) being hunted mercilessly by the lizards. Ah, Mother Nature. Such a cruel bitch, but so much fun to watch.

I turned my attention back to the house and admired the craftsmanship. It was built of stout beams and clad with thick cypress, all painted a dazzling white. This house could certainly (survive the gathering storm) stand for a hundred years or more.

I walked around the left, or westerly, side of the house. It was nearly impossible to walk around the eastern side unless you wanted to climb over the sprawling roots of the tree. I turned the corner to the back of the house and, for the first time, noticed the house was built on a slight hill. While the front had twenty steps up, the back had only three. I also noticed the electrical wires, mounted to a pole and stretching off into the surrounding scrub woods. I had a mind to follow those wires to see where they ended up, but for now, I hobbled up the three shorts steps and went into the big house.

I opened the plain, stout, wooden door and stepped into a mud room and then the pantry. It was cool and dim and I was glad to see plenty of supplies stocked up just like at the cottage. The pantry led into the kitchen and the kitchen naturally led to the dining room complete with a huge table and ten chairs. Off the kitchen was the parlor and the library and the stairs leading to the second floor. I looked at the stairs that nearly broke my leg last night and felt more than just a tingle of apprehension. What if I went up there and saw that poor little boy again? Or smelled the thick salty aroma of the ocean? Or heard the screams? Or the splash of a shark's tail? I stood and wondered about the terrors that lay in wait for me up those polished wooden stairs. I finally decided that the terror of not having a job was worse than anything my imagination could spin. I propped my crutch against the wall, grabbed the handrail and lugged up the stairs. My knee complained, but I told it to shut up and reached the landing. I looked around and all seemed to be in order. No dead bodies floated, no sharks swirled and no mangled little boys called to me. I nodded curtly and limped around, checking all the rooms. All was well and still, exactly as it should be. I (carefully this time) headed back down the stairs grasping the handrail. I reached for my crutch and realized that I was walking nearly fine and climbing down the stairs without it, so I carried it out the front door and chucked it back into the pile of lumber. I thought that since the workmen were apparently gone for good, it was up to me to clear that lumber pile. I resolved to do so first thing in the morning. That lumber pile got cleared soon enough, oh yes, but not by my hand.

I grabbed my ditty bag off the step. It didn't seem as if it was infested with any crawling things, so I slung it over my shoulder and limped back to the cottage. I looked out across the island and noticed that, even though the sun was shining hot and fierce, the sky was an angry purple way off in the distance to the west. Mrs. Howey was due to the island tomorrow afternoon and I hoped the storm passed before her boat arrived.

When I got to the cottage, I figgered that two beers was enough for the morning and brewed up a pot of coffee. While it burbled and sputtered in the percolator, I found a pencil and paper and started jotting down the things I had to accomplish before the guests of honor arrived. Mr. Howey had given me a piece of paper with lists of things to do, but I wanted to put them in an order that made sense to me. I had to pull all the dropcloths from the furniture, make up beds, clear any building lumber left behind and seed the front yard of the big house and plant Mrs. Howey's favorite flowers (plumeria) in front of the porch. Bags of seed and potted plants could be found inside of a shed behind the big house according to Mr. Howey's neat, flowing penmanship. I compared the two lists. Scratch that, the seeds and flowers could wait. Check under the beds for bugs or pests, flush the commodes and check the running water should come first. Ah, and the electricity. Here was the answer to the lines running off into the wooded area. On the northeastern side of the island was a circuit breaker built into a small shed. That made sense. The northeastern side of the island was the most protected and the closest to the mainland. The cables must run into the seabed and connect somewhere onshore to the power plant. I shook my head wondering how much it must have cost to run electricity that far. Well, Mr. Howey certainly had the money. If the power went out, I should open the shed and throw the circuit breaker connected to a large wooden handle. This should restore the power. The word "should" was not very comforting, nor was the idea of throwing a circuit breaker connected to wires that snaked under the ocean. There was a small diagram of a circuit breaker, shaped like a lower case "h" and a little lightning bolt next to it. Hmm. Well maybe the power will just stay on and I won't have to touch the thing.

The coffee pot hissed to let me know it was done so I got up and poured a steaming mug of it, black. My knee had stiffened up a bit, so I limped into the bathroom and rummaged around in the medicine cabinet for some aspirins. I found them, shook out three and chewed them up. They work faster that way. I washed the bitterness down with some coffee and sat back down to my list.

My tasks were simple enough for today: make the house ready for Mrs. Howey and the nurse that will be landing here with her. I wondered how they would make it off that little boat, on to shore and up the road to the house. It's a bit of a walk for fit men. Two women, one of them with child, may have a hard go of it. I also wondered, for the hundredth time, why on earth a man would send his pregnant wife out here, nearly alone save for a nurse and a caretaker with no experience, but that was not mine to wonder.

I looked at my list and decided to put Mrs. Howey's flowers right to the top. It wouldn't take long and it would be nice for her to see her favorites planted in front of the house. It might cheer her up after the long walk. A cool glass of ice tea would be in order too, so I put that on the list just under the flowers. My list in order, I folded it into my pocket, swallowed the last of my coffee and headed out of the cottage.

The shed was just where the list told me to find it. About a hundred yards behind the big house, cleverly hidden behind some tall bushes. I never even noticed it before, even though it was quite large. Made of rough planking and painted white like the house, it had two doors that opened outward and held closed by an opened padlock with the key in the keyhole. I pocketed the key, hung the lock on the hasp and swung the big doors open. It was stifling hot in there and I heard wasps buzzing up in the rafters. As long as they stayed up there where they belonged, I had no issue with them. If they decided to swarm down on me, well I guess I would take care of them the best way I knew how; by running the hell away on my bum knee.

I stood there for a moment surveying the contents and keeping a wary eye on the lazily buzzing wasps. They didn't seem to take much notice of me so I guessed it safe to step inside. There was a bunch of yard tools hanging on one wall; shovels, rakes, scythes, axes, large brooms and some sharp and pointy things the purpose of which I had no idea. There was two roller lawn mowers that you push and a cylindrical blade spins around, hacking grass and two big wagons for toting stuff around. There seemed to be enough tools for an entire crew of caretakers. Maybe I was supposed to use a tool until it wore out and then go grab a replacement. The thought of wearing out a steel shovel was a bit depressing, so I checked out the other walls. Here was stacked rods and reels for fishing and nets, and even a speargun. Propped up in one corner was a wooden row boat. The boat seemed big enough standing up in a shed, but it couldn't have been over ten foot long. Anyone who took a ten foot boat out into the water that surrounded this island was either desperate or crazy. The thought gave me a chill, and I hoped I never got enough of either to ever put that thing in the water. Leaning next to the boat was four wooden oars. In the middle of the shed was sacks of grass seed stacked chest high. I grunted when I saw them and realized I had quite a task ahead throwing that seed. The wagons were just about big enough for two sacks and pulling a wagon with that much weight would wear down a man stronger than me. Well, Mr. Howey wanted pretty grass all around the house so I guessed I would have to do it. Next to the seed were pots filled with all types of plants and flowers. I had no idea what a plumeria looked like and I had a dismal moment where I feared I might put the wrong flowers in the planting bed by the long porch. Then I noticed that the plants all had tags hanging off their stems or tied onto their pots. I got down on my haunches and saw mango and papaya, and kumquat and, of course, orange, lemon, lime and grapefruit. It seemed Mr. Howey wanted to make his island a grove. I saw crinum lily, and amaranthus, and tickseed and milkweed. This place had plenty of weeds already and probably ticks too, but I kept looking. I saw frangipani, paw-paws and bromeliads. The only thing that even sounded close to plumeria was wisteria. I pulled a wagon over, grabbed a wisteria and plopped it in. I reached down to move a frangipani out of the way and the label attached to a thin branch fell off. The last thing I wanted to do was mix these things up, so I picked up the label and noticed that other side had writing. Ah ha! On the flip side of the label was written "plumeria" I replaced the wisteria and loaded up the wagon with a dozen of frangipani. I pulled a brand-new shovel off the wall, placed it in the wagon next to the sweet, pungent flowers and trundled off with my load towards the big house.

When I looked towards the west, I was stunned to see that the dark purple that was on the horizon earlier had halved the distance to the island. I wondered how many flowers I could plant before I would have to seek shelter in the cottage and wait out the rain. Well, it might not be that bad. The rain would water the flowers and take the edge off the heat. If it was just a light rain, I could work through it and stay cool. I quickened my step anyway, eager to get as much done as soon as I could. My knee was feeling better and I hoped it wouldn't stiffen up too much as I dug holes and knelt to pat the dirt down around the plants.

I made it around the front of the big house and realized I didn't have nearly enough plants to fill the long planting bed. I decided to plant what I had and go back for more. It didn't matter anyway, because not one fancy plumeria/frangipani made it into the ground. I had stuck the shovel in the dirt all of two times before I heard a hum off in the distance. I stopped and cocked my head, trying to place the sound. I looked to the north, hoping that the electricity wasn't the source of the hum. I had no desire to throw that breaker and fry myself on my second day here. The sound kept growing and I turned towards the west. I shielded my eyes and there off in the distance I saw a white speck. The speck grew until it formed into the shape of a boat. I watched it for a moment and then turned back to my task. I had no time for sightseeing with a dozen and half, maybe more, flowers to plant. I slung a few more shovelfuls of dirt and eyed one of the plants. The hole looked about right, so I grasped the plant out of its pot and set it on the ground. I stood up to get a better grip and glanced out towards the water again. I was shocked to see that the boat was not only a lot closer, it was heading right to the inlet. I stared, confused because the boat was large. I wondered if some playboy fisherman was drunk, or lost or both. The boat slowed and heeled around until it was almost sideways with the island and just outside the shallow lagoon. At least the captain knew to not get beached in the shallow water. The boat finished its slow turn and I saw that it was large enough to have a small dinghy hanging off the back. A man was busy at the stern and it became apparent that he was lowering the little boat off into the water.

I had no idea who these people were, but I knew that I was the caretaker and trespassers were not welcome. I looked at the plants and my task ahead and decided that I did not have time for this intrusion. Still, I headed down the oiled road to the water, my shovel resting on my shoulder like a rifle; the only weapon I had handy, to meet the intruders. As I walked down the road, and I briefly lost sight of the water, it dawned on me that maybe the boat was not trespassing at all. I wondered if I got my days mixed up? Could Mrs. Howey and her nurse be on the boat? I chucked the shovel and aside and jogged as best as my knee would let me. As I rounded the curve and got sight of the water again, I realized I was right. The dinghy was now in the water, plowing through the waves toward the island and I could see two women and a driver in the back. I got to the beachlet and realized the the wind had picked up and the bruised sky was almost above us. Thunder rumbled and lightning flashed and the little boat bounced and bucked. Finally it made it to the shallows and I bounded out into the water up to my knees to grasp the bowline.

"Mrs. Howey! I didn't expect you until tomorrow!"

"There's a storm coming and my husband and the captain thought it would be a good idea if I got here before it hit. Looks like we just made it!"

I tugged the little boat up as far into the shallow water as I could. Mrs. Howey's nurse, grunting, handed me a huge suitcase and I trudged it up onto the sand, holding it above my head to keep it out of the water. I walked back to the boat and told Mrs. Howey that she's probably going to get a bit wet. I couldn't pull the boat any closer.

She laughed "I've been wet before, and I'll be wet again, I'm sure"

She reached out and I grabbed her hand as she held her full belly and gingerly stepped off the boat into the water. It only came halfway up her shin. I was glad she only got her shoes wet and not her whole dress. I guided her to the sand and heard "Ahem" behind me and turned to see the nurse with her hand out. I mumbled "Sorry ma'am" and reached out to steady her way off the boat. She plopped into the water with a splash, soaking both of us and she grunted her disapproval as she passed by me, yanking her hand out of mine. Mrs. Howey just smiled and looked at the cemetery and then the road.

"Where's this fancy house Howey promised me?"

"Just up the road, ma'am"

I grabbed her bag and beckoned her to follow me.

As we trudged up the oiled road, the storm threatened overhead. Thunder boomed and lightening flashed. The wind whipped the ladies hair around and despite their best efforts, they could not keep it from crazily swirling around their heads. I looked back at the nurse and stuck out my hand to her.

"I'm the caretaker, ma'am".

"Name's Delores, and don't call me ma'am.

"Yes, ma'... Delores it is"

We hurried up the road to the big house and I was amazed at how dark the day had become. The storm was upon us and big, fat raindrops started pelting us. Slowly at first, they came and then quickly swept at us sideways. We kept our heads down and Mrs. Howey and Delores only glanced briefly at the mausoleum. When we reached the house, I limped up the steps ahead of the women, lugging the suitcase, Mrs. Howey asked if I was okay. I said of course, I'm fine ma'am, why do you ask? She said "You're limping".

I said I'm fine, just twisted my knee. I set the suitcase down and opened the door wide for the women to enter. Mrs. Howey took a few steps in and admired the house. I uttered,

"Sorry I haven't got the house ready. I meant to remove the drop cloths and make the beds, but I thought you wouldn't be here tomorrow so I started to plant your flowers and then you got here and the storm..." I trailed off.

She looked at me with a sweet smile and told me it was fine. Delores could help with the sheets get the house ready. After all, it was still early and this was just a summer storm. I mumbled "Yes ma'am" and headed towards the stairs with the big suitcase. My Lord, there must be clothes in here for half a dozen women. I clomped across the floor, lugging the suitcase and Mrs. Howey touched my shoulder.

"First of all, stop with the "Ma'am" business, call me Marty. Secondly, what's your name?"

I mumbled "Jedidiah Johnson"

Mrs. Howey had a sparkle in her bright green eyes.

"So they call you Jedidiah?"

"No ma'am..um. Marty. No, they call me JJ for short."

Marty covered a giggle with the back of her hand while Delores sighed and rolled her eyes.

"I suspected that you had a nickname. In fact, I already knew it."

I gaped at her like an idiot.

"Of course, silly. You don't think my husband told me the name of the man who was looking after me?"

Delores bitched and fussed and moaned while Mrs. Howey looked at me with a steady gaze and I felt my good knee go weak and my bum knee give out for a second and I stumbled a bit. I saw the little spray of freckles across her nose and her lips turned up in a little smile. Not derisive, but welcoming and knowing. Her hair, long and brown with droplets of rain clinging wafted her smell towards me. I couldn't quite place the scent at first, but then it dawned on me. Frangipani. Her favorite flower somehow captured in a bottle and gently wrapped around her person. Unconsciously, I lifted my hand and rubbed my chin and smelled the plumeria (frangipani) I had been planting before she, and the storm landed here on Howey's Island. Of course she would know my name. She probably knew all about me and my wife and boy and the little house we rented from her husband. Mr. Howey would have surely told her everything. My face turned red and I felt like a teenager caught in the woods with my pants down and my dick in my hand. I stammered "Of course Mrs. Marty" and she giggled again. Her sweet laugh was the tinkle of fairies dancing on the rim of glasses filled with liquid happiness.

I tried to drag my gaze from those eyes, those green liquid pools of delight, and mumbled something about getting her clothes upstairs just as a flash of lightning blazed like the sun and a second later the house shook with thunder. Both women squealed and I started, as if from a dream, and the severity of the storm hit me like a ten ton heavy thing. All three of us turned to the windows as the wind howled and the rain pelted the side of the house. I said, best to get upstairs and lay low til the storm passes, ladies. How wrong I was, Dear Lord, how wrong I was.

We headed up the stairs, me limping the lead, Marty behind me (I sincerely hoped my unperfumed ass didn't smell too bad) and Delores bringing up the rear. We reached the landing and I caught a whiff of salt water rich with the smell of clams and crabs and other sea things and I shook it off. No time for hallucinations now. It was my job to take care of these women and that's exactly what I intended to do. I warily looked in the corner, expecting to see the little boy, but the corner was empty.

"C'mon JJ" barked Delores. "We don't have all day!"

I led the women to the master suite and set the suitcase down by the foot of the unmade bed. Delores huffed and puffed and banged open closets and dressers in her search for clean sheets. Marty looked in the bathroom and then the nursery. She stood there for a moment just taking it all in. She finally shook her head once and said

"It's a girl. He painted it the wrong color" Our eyes met as the wind went from a howl to a scream and the branch from the banyan tree crashed into the side of the house, shattering the window and tearing off part of the wall and connecting roof. The rain poured in like buckets as Delores' head was lopped off by the branch as neatly as if a guillotine had sliced it. Gouts of blood squirted from her neck as she crumpled to the floor. Marty screamed and I screamed and she tripped and fell into the nursery. In my terror, I looked out of the hole in the house and saw the branches of the banyan tree whipping back and forth like a thing alive. A vine cracked above my head like a bullwhip, the air sizzling as it nearly took my own head. The sound was drowned out by another gigantic crash of thunder with a simultaneous flash of lightning. I counted mindlessly one one thousand and knew the storm was directly upon us. Time slowed to a crawl and I remembered my grandpa, smelly from too few baths and too many roll your owns and too many cups of coffee. I sat on his lap on the porch and we counted the seconds between lightning and thunder and we knew how far the storm was from us. One one second was one mile. Usually a storm was at least three one thousands away. I laid my head on his bony shoulder and drifted off into a five year old boy's dream land. Safe, warm and dry, I rode muscular horses through rich pastures, I fought Vikings on stout ships and I worked the levers of smoking, hissing locomotives through narrow mountain passes. The brief day(night)dream was shattered when another branch was torn from the mighty banyan outside. I twisted, trying to dodge the huge branch and my knee gave out for good. My bum knee probably saved my miserable life because I went down. Hard. the branch crashed through what was left of the outside wall and landed solid against the nursery door. Marty cried out "JJ help me. The door is stuck." I got up supporting myself on the wet branch that had no business in this no nonsense, expertly crafted house. I yelled to Marty I would get her out, don't worry, don't fret.

I crawled over the branch (hah branch...this was a fucking tree) and wrapped my arms around it, pulling on the wet bark. I couldn't even reach all the way around it. I yelled to Marty again HANG ON while I furiously thought of how to get in the nursery and get her out before this cursed tree destroyed the entire house. My mind fell short of a solution. The room was on the second floor. It had one door, blocked by the tree, and one small window. The half a little boy drifted by in a slow eddy and he admonished me "You never helped me, you bad man" I screamed that I was not a bad man. "I'm doing the best I can" Tears streamed down my face, washed away by the rain. I wiped my face and it came away bloody. I had no idea that I even been cut. The shark cruised around me in slow, lazy circles, getting closer and closer by every turn. In my terror, I threw myself into the bathroom and slammed the door. Marty's voice, as if in my ear said "...are you there?" I assured her I was and would get her out. I looked around the bathroom. Incredibly, the lights were still on. I felt a surge of relief that I wouldn't have to throw the breaker and saw exactly what I needed. I grabbed the porcelain lid off the commode and started pounding on the wall. The plaster let loose in huge chunks and I saw the lath underneath. Knowing I was almost halfway through, I redoubled my efforts. A chunk broke off the lid and that was good because now the lid was sharp, like an axe. I pounded on the lath and broke through between two studs and saw the lath of the other side. I shattered those and the plaster attached and finally saw Marty. I told her to back away and I cleared the last of the lath and plaster on her side. There was another crash as another huge branch broke free in the fury of the wind and rain. We looked at each other through the broken wall. Her green eyes were worried, but still pools of calm.

She simply said
"Help me" and then incredibly, she smiled.

I reached through the gap and took her hand and pulled. She allowed me to pull her towards me, never for a second did her eyes leave mine. As her body reached the gap, we both realized that her belly, full with her little girl, would not fit through the beams. I told her to wait and let her hand go. I pounded against the stout cypress studs that Mr. Howey so thoughtfully demanded be installed. The studs budged not an inch. Not with the pathetic I toilet lid I was swinging. I looked through the gap at her, and she at me and we both knew she would never leave that room alive. She reached out her hand to me and her lips formed the words "I'm sorry" I screamed something incomprehensible just as the banyan tree let loose of its roots and crashed through the rest of the house like a conquered giant.

The storm whipped and howled and lashed the island for twelve hours or more. Even the weathermen and all their fancy doodads never saw the hurricane coming. Weathermen are supposed to be scientists, but they're more like fake swamis trying to guess the future with a crystal ball. I've never trusted either. They say the storm with no name hit faster than any hurricane in recorded history. They may be right about that part, at least, because that storm came up on the island in a blink and destroyed everything along with an ancient tree and more than one man's hopes and dreams.

They also said that the storm destroyed all their instruments just before they clocked the winds at one hundred and ninety miles per hour.

Early the next day, long before the weathermen spouted their opinions and statistics and before the newspapers printed their grim stories, I woke up in the woods beyond the slight rise in the ground. It was peaceful and quiet except for the birds singing their morning song and the crickets wrapping up their night song. The sun was not yet full up on the horizon and I laid there sleepily remembering the nightmare. I sat up quickly, and felt a throbbing pain in my head; a familiar feeling here on the island. I realized that the lower half of my body was lying in a puddle. I had to pee so I got up and the events of last night hit me like a brick wall. I looked around, trying to get my bearings. I saw a massive pile of white cedar lumber and furniture and a stove perched precariously on top of the tangle with a lone wall attached to it in one direction and my cottage in another. I unzipped my pants and let loose a long stream. As I peed, the reality struck me. Mrs. Howey (Marty) was dead. Delores was dead. I was still alive, so I slowly zipped up, stood against a leaning, crooked tree and weeped, my tears dripping into a muddy puddle. I weeped until I realized that Marty might still be alive. As I hobbled towards the pile of house that was crushed by the enormous tree, I scolded myself for my selfishness. I screamed "MARTY! DELORES! ANYONE?!

I clambered over the parts of the fallen tree. I could see the remnants of the big house crushed under the weight of a tree that was nearly as big as the house itself. I grabbed boards and threw them aside. I grabbed the fancy front door, now cracked and mangled and I screamed "Marty?" "Delores?" until my throat was sore and coarse. By the time the sun started to blister the morning I knew that they were lost. Likely swept out to sea in an angry, unrelenting wave. Hopefully dashed upon a branch or a beam or the hard soil before they had to suck the ocean into their lungs. I clambered down from the wreckage that was to be the Williams Family Manor.

I limped to my cottage, that was, incredibly, spared destruction and sat at the sopping kitchen table. The front door was gone and the windows shattered. Everything in the cottage was soaked. I hung my head in shock and sorrow. I stood up and hobbled over to the icebox. I opened the door and took out a beer. The bottle hissed as the cap fell off. It went down cold and good, a small consolation in the face of such suffering and destruction. Disgusted, I hurled the bottle, unfinished against the wall. It didn't even have the decency to shatter. It just thumped against the wall and hit the floor, its remaining contents sadly dribbling out. As I watched the beer spill out, I heard an engine burbling off in the distance so I hurried outside as fast as I could. The big boat with the dinghy on the back that delivered Mrs. Howey (Marty) to her destiny cruised just off the shallows. I can't say for sure that I saw Mr. Howey survey the damage through binoculars and instruct the captain to turn around and head for the mainland, but that's exactly what the big boat did, leaving me behind.

I stayed on the island, looking for something; anything. Any small trace of Marty. While I searched, I kept expecting another boat to motor up with a rescue party. No boat ever showed up and the days turned into weeks. The electricity was gone, but there was still plenty of supplies. I boarded up the windows in the cottage and made a makeshift door from the wreckage of the big house. The shed was gone, tools tossed and strewn about, and I assumed that the little boat was washed out to sea. Every day I scoured the wreckage of William's Manor. Climbing over the twisted and broken lumber and under the ancient, fallen banyan tree, I found nothing. Not even the shattered little boy, nor the old lady or the shark bitten woman or a trace of Marty and Delores' suitcase. It was as if they had never even been here. I was totally alone on the island. The storm had apparently washed away even the ghosts that I was previously convinced I saw.

I suppose my wife and son thought the hurricane had washed me away because they never sent anyone for me. There were lonely nights and long days spent wondering how they were and if they ever had a thought of me. I finally realized that I must be dead to them.

Three days after finally running out of food, I headed off into the woods to look for berries or maybe a lizard to catch and eat. I was shocked to find the little rowboat, tangled upside down in a bunch of thick vines. I dragged the boat out of the woods after cutting the vines away and set it down near the cottage. I had seen a paddle near the wreckage of the shed and headed off to look for it. I found the paddle and shovel that would serve as a makeshift oar and realized that I would now have to paddle across that rough gulf to the mainland. It was a terrifying thought, but starving to death was worse. I went back to the cottage with my mismatched oars. I flipped the boat right side up, tossed in the oar and the shovel and dragged the boat down the path to the beachlet. I gazed out across the choppy water to the mainland off in the distance. I wasn't sure if I could make it, but I knew I definitely wouldn't if I didn't put the boat in the water and at least try.

I pushed the boat into the water, chocked the oar and the shovel into the oarlocks and put my back into rowing. I'm not sure how long it took me to get within shouting distance of the little fishing town on the mainland, but it felt like at least a few lifetimes. My shoulders were wooden from the strain and I could barely move my arms.

The man who ran the crab shack stood on his dock and watched me make my way over the waves. He looked at me like I was crazy, which I suppose, in a way, I was. When I got close enough he threw me a line and

I grabbed it and gratefully pulled the little dinghy up to the dock. He looked and me asked did I paddle all the way from the island? I nodded that yes, I did. I asked if he had any food and water to spare for a hungry man with no money and he supposed that he did. After I wolfed down two bowls of thick fish chowder and drank my fill of coffee, I asked him if there was any way to get a ride into town. He looked at me with his head tilted to the side and I explained that if he gave me a ride to my house, I would gladly pay him for the chowder and coffee.

We piled into his rusty old pickup and left a trail of blue smoke as we bounced and jostled toward to my house. I was excited, and a bit nervous, to see my family. I hoped they didn't have too much of a shock opening the door to what they thought was a dead man.

We pulled up to the house with the overgrown yard and for rent sign out front and the crabber looked at me. I asked him to kindly wait a moment. I slowly walked up the path and cupped my face to the window. The little house was empty and dusty and I could see cobwebs in the corners. I went back to the chugging and farting pickup and the old man asked if mayhap I had the wrong address. I shook my head and said I'm sorry I don't have your money, but thank you for the ride and the meal. I started to walk away and the truck lurched forward on its worn out clutch and the man waved for me to get in.

We got back to his crab shack and he offered me a baker's dozen of crabs in a brown paper sack. I said thank you, and accepted and asked if I could bother him for a ride back to the island. He obliged and added some bread and cider to the sack and motored me back to the island, towing my little rowboat behind his skiff.

The years went by like the tides and the crab man always picked me up and took me back every few days, never asking a question other than the clouds look heavy today. Think it'll rain? I never opined whether I thought it would or not because the heavy clouds did what they wanted and I had no say in the matter.

Mr. Howey never did come back to get buried in his mausoleum. Still, I pulled the weeds and raked the leaves around it and kept it neat. I fashioned a cross of driftwood and carefully carved Marty and Baby into it with my pocketknife. I stuck it in the ground next to the mausoleum and planted some wildflowers around it. They weren't Marty's favorites, but it was the best I could do. I thought she would probably understand. I also made a cross for Delores, and kept it neat and tidy too. It was my only real task and I took it seriously.

The crab man must have died sometime last week or got tired of his every other day trip to the island to bring me crabs and water and cigarettes and even a few beers now and then. Likely he was dead. He was old when he first threw me that line and I can't even remember how long ago that was. I'm too hungry and tired to row the old little boat back to the mainland again. It's been leaking bad anyway and likely to sink if it's put on deep water.

So here I sit, an old used up man, the last survivor of this wretched swath of land stuck in the ocean, yet frustratingly within sight of land, smoking my last Camel.

What's left of the cemetery of the empty and broken to my right, My lost family and my vision of Marty to my back and the gathering storm directly ahead of me. The sky is purple and angry off in the horizon. I'm not sure I'll survive this storm and I'm pretty sure I don't want to.

By now the girls had gathered around and the three of us looked at our friend; stunned at the story he had just told. My girl giggled nervously, snuggled closer to me and said it was all surely made up. A salty ghost story. When she said that, a shiver went up my spine and I noticed that the temperature had dropped. The afternoon storms that were on the horizon earlier were uncomfortably close. Dark, swiftly moving clouds had started to block out the sun. My friend said we should haul anchor and haul ass out of here to beat the storm. We all agreed and made ready to leave. Once everything was secured, he pushed the throttle to it's stop and turned the boat around, churning the water into a trail of white that we tried to outrun. Holding on to the console, I glanced back at the island. I swore I saw an old man stand up from the sand, flick his cigarette into the surf, turn and walk away.

THE MASTER KEY

I sang,

> *"Hey Mr. Tambourine Man, play a song for me.*
> *I'm not sleepy and there is no place I'm going to".*

I didn't have a tambourine, but Dylan songs usually got bigger tips. Something about the folksy sound resonated with the businessmen and women that passed.

> *"Hey Mr. Tambourine man, play a song for me,*
> *in the jingle-jangle morning*
> *I'll come following you".*

The suits that threw quarters and, sometimes dollars, in my guitar case have mostly never heard a jingle-jangle song before and probably wouldn't know Bob Dylan from Bob Dole, but they gave me money and that meant food, sometimes smokes and every once in awhile, a bottle or two of beer. So, Bob Dylan it was.

Name's Mike. If I had any friends they'd call me Mickey. I'd like to tell you that I get by with a little help from my friends, but that would be a lie and there's no reason to start off tellin' a fib. I've been on the streets playing music for, I think, about a few years or maybe ten.

I don't have a calendar or a smart-ass phone and I don't want neither. I like it out here. There's no bosses, there's no wives and I make my own schedule. I mostly play the songs I wanna play. But, I will play the songs that bring the most tips. "Knockin' on Heaven's Door" is one of my personal favorites, but the dollars turn to quarters, so I save that one for later in the day. I like "The Joker" too and some people like it, some people hate it, so I try it out and see what it pulls. If it pulls some coin, I finish it out, if not, I go back to the jingly-jangly. Man's gotta eat, right? Anyways, I keep my guitar tuned. She's old, but trusty and even with worn out strings, she sings like that was what she was made for. I have an old pitch pipe that helps her stay pretty sounding. If you don't know what a pitch pipe is, it's basically a round harmonica. Now, you're not supposed to play it like a harmonica, but I suppose you could if you wanted to. Like I said, it's round, about the size of a beer bottle bottom and it plays notes when you blow into it. That's how I keep my pretty stringy lady in tune. Blow an E note through the pitch pipe, stretch the E string up to match. On to the next string. Simple. Do that six times and the little lady sings and puts food in my belly. Nobody, even the yuppies wishing they were hippies, will pay a nickel for a song outta tune. At least that's what I thought.

So one day, it's raining and nasty out. I'm hangin out in the park under a tree tuning up. Right by this tree is a sewer grate. It smells like a dead man's ass down there, but it's sorta dry under the tree. So I'm blowing a fat ol' B note and my pitch pipe slips right outta my wet hand, bounces across the grass and rolls, pretty as you please, down into the sewer grate. I could not have planned it any better if I tried. I stood there, looking at my pitch pipe get sucked into the rushing rain water, and my heart drops. My heart is never really all that high anyways these days, but this sight makes it drop another notch. That notch is somewhere between despair and screw it, I'm giving up. I've had it with this shit. But, I think of the jingly-janglies and the dollars falling into my open guitar case and I say what the hell. I've got four strings tuned, I can tune the rest by ear. So I set about trying to find that elusive B note. B is always a pain in my ass. It warbles and changes and sounds in tune and then not. It's just B. There's something about the half-note, which I don't understand, but just feel. Anyways, I get the B just about right and move on to the high E. It warbles and screeches, but it sounds almost ok.

I put the old girl away in her case, to keep her sorta dry, and head down the street to my corner. There's an overhang there, which kinda keeps me dry, and I open my case, take out my guitar and start off with "Rockin' in the Free World". It's not by Dylan, but Neil Young is close enough. A thousand points of light and so forth. It's an ironic song and the dollars start flowing. Something doesn't quite sound right, but I keep on playing and before I know it, the dollars are turning to fives. I'm looking at the pile of bills in my case with amazement. There's not even any change at all, just ones and fives. I finish the song and start in on "Blowin' in the Wind". That one's never been one of the favorites, so I switch over to Steve Miller Band,

> *"I'm a picker, I'm a grinner,*
> *I'm a lover and I'm a sinner".*

The song is flowin'. It's not one of my money

makers, and the poor old girl is obviously out of tune, but the fives and now even tens are dropping in my old battered case. I catch a groove on the song and my ooohs and my wooohhooohs are dripping like honey off my lips. I finish up;

"Sure don't want to hurt no one".

Before I knew it, the skies had cleared. It stopped raining, but it was humid, and the sun was setting. I blinked and looked around at the streets that were nearly empty. It didn't make any sense. I only played three songs. I flexed my hands and fingers and looked at the callouses that years of playing had built up. There was deep grooves in my fingertips that screamed I had been playing all day, not just three songs. I shook it off, must be catching the dementia that runs like a scared rat out here on the streets. I scooped up the money in my case, figgerin I had easily over a weeks take in one day. I shook my head again and gently put my baby in her case, shut the clasps, grabbed the tape-wrapped handle and headed down the street.

I was hungry. Nothin' new there. But today, I had a pocketful of cash money. I turned my heel and headed up to an avenue that I knew had a Cuban Cantina that stayed open late. For five bucks you could get a big bowl of rice and refried beans or six bucks would get you a pressed Cuban sandwich full of meat with a side of long-sliced pickles. My mouth watered as I thought about a real meal, my first in about a week. Sure, I could get a hot dog from the street vendor. She was sweet and usually threw in some chips and a soda for the price of just a dog. Buck fifty. Not bad, but I could only afford one, maybe two a day. Plus, I didn't wanna take advantage of her. Phyliss, or was it

Paula? Can't remember, but either way, I didn't wanna get somethin for nothin. God knows, I might need her generosity another day when the dollars were thin and the coins lonely.

Tonight my dollars were fat so I walked with purpose down the grimy, angled street. I must have went too far, or not far enough, because there was no Cantina here. I looked over my shoulder and back ahead and realized I was halfway down the street so I made me an executively decision and went forward. I saw a pool of light on the sidewalk and made that my goal. Maybe I had the right street after all. As I got closer, I saw I was mistaken. This was not an eatery, this was a junky shop that wanted to be much more important someday. Maybe An Antique Shoppe when it grew up. But for now, and probably when the doors were chained shut and the windows soaped over, it would be a junk shop until it wheezed its last breath.

I walked up to the grimy windows and thought maybe this place already wheezed its last. The window was filmed over with that kinda dirt you only see deep in the city. Black from truck exhaust and looking like it had never been cleaned. Except the parts where somebody pressed their face against the glass to have a closer look. Cobwebs in the corner, a pathetic display of old, creepy dolls, a typewriter that looked like it's last article was something about the Nazis marching across Poland and, wait. I moved closer, my hands cupping the dirty window. I got a big, black smudge on my nose that I didn't even notice until later. I guess I cleaned my own face-shaped part of the glass. There in the corner was a Master Key Pitch Pipe. It was sitting there, pretty as you please, in it's red plastic case, nestled in fake blue velvet. I stepped back and looked deeper into the shop. The was an old man sitting on a stool, his chin resting on his chest, a thin drizzle of drool dripping right into his shirt pocket. Snoozing the day, and now the night away. I went to the door, which was a bit inset from the storefront and turned the knob. Fool. Don't waste your dollars in a junky shop. That money in your pocket meant food for days. But yet, I had to tune my guitar didn't I? I might not have another lucky day like today. Gotta plan for the future and my future meant belting out the Dylan songs. In tune.

I twisted the old knob and nothing happened. Right, left. pushed, pulled. Well, maybe they were closed and the old man dozed off before turning out the lights. I looked one more time at the old pitch pipe and decided it was for best anyway. I turned and walked away. I got ten steps from the door when I heard a click and the jingle-jangle of a bell. I turned around and saw the old man standing there, door open. He coughed, and bent over a bit and made a wet, whooping sound like his lungs were going to just hack right out onto the sidewalk. I was a bit worried for the old guy, but I kept my distance and my mouth shut. Best to not get involved into someone else's hacking fit. Never know what ya might catch. I heard there's the tooberlocus out here in places. Ya know? The locomotive breath? He spat a huge gob of throat snot and croaked

"Help ya?"
I said, "Umm"

He opened the door wide and told me to come on in and look around. I looked down the street both ways and my belly argued about that pressed Cuban sandwich. I could smell the stale odor of the shop wafting out. It was the smell of old man farts, musty corners filled with dead spider webs, and dust that had probably been there longer than I've been alive. The scent was swept away on the humid breeze and I felt myself turning towards the door, tripping a bit over the threshold and then I was inside. The door closed with a rattly jangle and I looked around. The place was crammed full of old radios, piles of clothes that went out of fashion around the last time a President got shot, doodads, cracked coffee cups and wall art that looked like it belonged in a motel where a killer on the road might stay and the stuff in the window case.

"Help Ya?" he said again.

I swallowed and said as a matter of fact, I'm kinda interested in the pitch pipe in the window. He said, yes, that was a mighty fine item, would I care to see it? He looked at the guitar case in my hand and then up at my forehead and said again that it was a mighty fine item, especially for a man like me. I wasn't really sure what that meant by that, but I nodded and mumbled that, sure, if it wasn't too much trouble, I wouldn't mind just a look. He reached far into the case; I thought he might just tumble right in there and out through the window. I reached out to steady his elbow, and quick as a cockroach, he was standing right up in front of me, the pipe cupped in both hands like it was the Holy Grail. I reached out to take it from him, a bit creeped out that he didn't just hand it to me. Before I knew what was happening he put the thing to his cracked old lips and played the harmonica part of "Times They Are a Changin." White spittle bubbled out of the corner of his mouth, and while I was somewhat horrified, I was also amazed. I always knew you could play a pitch pipe like a harmonica, but I had never seen nobody do such a thing. He removed the pipe from his lips, swiped his hand across his mouth and handed the slobbery thing to me. He must have seen the look of disgust on my face and wiped the pitch pipe off on his smelly shirt.

I took it in my hand and looked at it. It was black on one side and chromey silver on the other. The black side had "CHROMATIC PITCH INST. MASTER-KEY etched into the surface along with the notes that matched the holes in the edge. I turned it this way and that and looked at it on edge. The notes seemed to line up right with the blow-holes, and while it was old, it was in pretty decent shape. My eyes met his and he suggested that I try it. I was still repulsed by his slobbery display, but I raised it to my lips and blew a gloriously accurate B note. I wanted to take my guitar out at that moment and tune it to this amazing little instrument, but I stayed calm and asked "How much?".

The old man pursed his lips, looked over his shoulder as if consulting an invisible business partner and looked back at my forehead. He slowly tapped his lips and a string of spittle connected from his lip to his finger. I watched with fascination as the string of spittle stretched, contracted, drooped, then stretched and finally broke free to rest on his grizzled chin.

He told me that this was a special item, perhaps the finest item in the shop. He said the he got it from Mudpuddle Slim long around '67 or '68. Seems Mudpuddle hit a bad patch and sold it for a song. He asked if I ever heard of the bluesman. I said of course. Mudpuddle Slim played with Robert Johnson back in the 30's There's rumor that just before Johnson died at age 27 from being poisoned by a jealous husband, him and Mudpuddle wrote "Whole Lotta Love" which Led Zeppelin made into a monster rock hit in 1969. I also knew that Mudpuddle Slim died in 1950, supposedly from a heart attack, but some say cocaine, so there was no way the old man got the pipe from Mudpuddle in '67 or '68. I kept my mouth shut and just nodded, waiting for a price. He said he could let it go for twenty five dollars. I knew I was getting worked, so I mumbled that it wasn't what I was looking for, thanked him for his time and turned to go. As I reached out for the doorknob his bony hand dropped on my shoulder. Ya know how when another person touches you, you're kinda amazed how warm they are? Well, his hand was cold. I could feel it through my shirt, all knobbly and bony and chilly. Like ice cubes wrapped in flesh. I cringed a bit and he told me to not be so hasty. After all, the customer always came first. He asked what I would offer? I shrugged a bit, mostly to get his claw off my shoulder. He suggested that maybe I should look in my pocket and see what I had to spend. I reached into my pocket and pulled out a wad of bills. I looked at the money stupidly, suddenly forgetting how to math. He told me that exact amount would do nicely and I handed the wad of cash to him. He bent over into the display window and I, again, reached out to steady him. He came out of the display window and handed me the case for the pipe. With numb fingers, I placed the pipe in the case, a perfect square for a perfect circle. I mumbled a thank you as he led me to the door, his bony fingers wrapped around my elbow.

Next thing I knew, I was outside in the warm night. The old man farts washed from my nostrils by the breeze once again. I heard the door click locked behind me. I turned to look back at the shop and the lights were already off. I looked at the display window, which was utterly empty except for a faded for rent sign. I cupped my hands to the window and saw a nearly empty space with a dusty floor and a single display case tipped over on its side, the glass shattered and strewn across the floor. I shook my head, knowing full well the dementia had grabbed me by the brain.

I once again looked up and down the street, trying to get my bearings. I saw the dawn light rising blue and lazy hazy in the east and wondered where the night had gone. Ran off with the day, I supposed. I headed towards the sun, knowing that my park bench, and the hot dog cart was that way. I had a few hours before the hot dog girl set up shop, but I was hungry right now. I reached in my pocket and my fingers wrapped around the pitch pipe. My gut clenched when I realized I had spent my entire windfall on a trinket and had no money for food. I trudged up the street and realized that dementia also meant going hungry.

I stopped by my bench and briefly considered a short nap. I felt like I had been up for days. I mentally shook my head and thought I could maybe scrape up a few bucks early and get a hot dog. So I headed to my corner, opened my guitar case and brought the old girl out. I strummed the strings and grimaced, wondering how I could have possibly made any money yesterday with a guitar tuned up sounding like a sick whale. I reached in my pocket and pulled out the pitch pipe. My new Master Key. I carefully removed it from it's case and blew that perfect, cool B note. The old girl's body rested on my knee and her neck in my left hand. I let go of her neck and gently turned the tuning key and made her sing with the pitch pipe. The thing tasted like the old man's breath smelled. A mixture of rotted fish, tobacco and dust. But, the note was pure and clean. I moved on to the high E note and barely noticed the flutter of a bill in my case. I looked down and saw a one hundred dollar bill. I chuckled to myself. Yea, I'm for sure losing it. I'm thinking ones are hundreds. As I turned the tuning key and looked at the intersection next to my corner, I saw the man who dropped the bill standing there looking at me with yellow eyes with vertical slits that blinked sideways. He was wearing an obviously expensive suit and he winked at me as the light turned green. Problem is, his wink was sideways. I sighed, and pocketed the buck, can't be too careful - if you get distracted, a thief will raid your case - it's happened to me before. I briefly wondered why a businessman (with lizard eyes) would be up with the sun, but that was no concern of mine. It was early and I had nearly enough for a dog and that was good enough for me. I had started tuning ass middle backwards, starting with the B string, so I moved to the low E and began tuning my sweety all proper like. As I moved through the strings, I heard the clickety-clack of high heels and glanced up to see a long, cool woman in a black dress heading my way. Click, clack went her heels, problem was, she didn't have no heels on and the sound was her sharp claws on the sidewalk. Click. Clack. I looked up at her green eyes and furry ears poking out of her perfectly hair-sprayed mane. She stopped in front of my case and looked at me with those cool, green eyes. She blinked and I noticed long, thin whiskers poking out of her face.

She said "Well?"

I blinked back at her.

"Are you going to play me a song or just sit there?" I was done tuning up so I just nodded and strummed an A chord and then a E and then a G. I played through the song and when I got to the verse:

"And in the evening when the sun is sinkin' low
Everybody's with the one they love
I walk the town, keep a-searchin' all around
Lookin' for my street corner girl"

She told me that was enough and rummaged around in her purse. Her paw came out grasping a bill. As she dropped the money in my case, she smiled. I briefly saw her rough tongue poke out and lick her pointy teeth. She gracefully turned and click-clacked away, her soft toepads trading places with her claws. As she stopped at the intersection to wait for the walk signal, her tail swished impatiently.

I was a bit baffled, to say the least. I was never much for playing Led Zeppelin songs, yet I made it almost all the way through one of their B-side hits. And, I earned a buck for my trouble. I thought maybe I might change up my song list a bit. Just for some flavor, ya know? Either way, I had enough now for a hot dog. I scooped up the bill and stared at Benjamin Franklin's face for a second and pocketed the money. I hoped Pam had her cart set up and then it dawned on me that the sun was on the wrong side of the sky. Traffic was light and there were few people on the sidewalk. In fact, as I glanced up and down the block, I only saw one guy in janitors overalls loping along on all fours, his stubbly tail twitching back and forth. I grabbed my case and headed towards Patty's hot dog cart.

A block from the cart, I could see she was packing up. I yelled "Penny, wait up". She looked up at me, put her hands on her ample hips and shook her head.

She said, "Mickey, I'm mostly sold out, but I
got two dogs left. You can have them"
"Forget about it, darlin', I got money today"

She said ok, whatever and started fixin' me two
dogs the way I like em. Lots of relish (gotta have your
veggies) lots of onions (gotta have your flavor) and brown
mustard cause ketchup is for kiddies at the ballpark.
I reached into my pocket, pulled out my two bucks and
handed them to her. She looked at the money and said,
"Are you kidding me? I don't got no change for
that."
I said "Keep the change, sweety, besides it's not
even enough for two dogs. Can you spot me a
soda?"
She snatched the money out of my hands and held up a
bill right in front of my face. I saw the face of Franklin
looking back at me. One hundred dollars. She switched the
bills like a magician doin a cheap trick and I saw Franklin
again. What the ever loving hell was going on? I must have
spoken out loud without realizing it cause she said "I dunno.
You tell me. Don't matter, take your money and your hot
dogs and get outta here". She crammed the hot dogs in my
left hand and the money in my right and pushed me away.

I mumbled something stupid and walked away as
she bustled her cart closed and pushed it away with a grunt.
I wandered over to a bench and sat down hard. Could this
be true? Did I really have two hundred dollars and two hot
dogs? If so, it was the most money I'd had in my pocket,
and the most food, at one time in a long time. I stuffed my

first dog in my mouth, bit off a goodly chunk and chewed thoughtfully. The onions were good and potent like they always were and I wished I had a drink of soda to wash it all down. I sat there, finished the first dog, and then the second and pondered my predicament. When I was done, I knew one thing: I was damn thirsty. I was also a bit sweaty and nervous and scared to look at the money in my pocket. I got up and headed to the liquor store down the avenue. If I was right or wrong, I had at least two bucks. That would get me a little nipper of whiskey, The whiskey wouldn't exactly help my thirst, but it would get me right. For a bit anyways.

I pulled the glass door open. No jingle nor jangle here. Everything was recorded on video, no need for a bell. I stepped up to the counter and asked the man for a small bottle of whisky and while he looked at me a bit sideways, he produced the bottle. I handed him a bill and he looked at me with suspicion, whipped a pen out of his pocket and made a stroke across the bill. Satisfied, he huffed and puffed and handed me ninety four dollars and sixty eight cents change. I know that was the zact amount because he counted it out into my hand by the last penny. I stood there like a moron and he asked if that was all and I said nope. "Can I have a cold cola too?" He told me I could by slapping the chilled can on the counter and taking a single dollar bill, a nickel and two pennies from the change in my hand that he had just made. I pocketed the rest of the money, grabbed up the cola and the whiskey and left the store.

I made my way to my bench and sat down hard. I twisted the cap off the whiskey and downed half of it in one swallow. I peeled the tab off of the soda and gulped down a goodly amount, producing a resonating belch that sounded somewhere near an F sharp and a B flat, which is all the same, thank you very much.. The drink made me sleepy, so I curled up on the bench, fell asleep and dreamed.

My wife and my little boy played on the grass while I squirted lighter fluid on the barbeque. I laughed as he tried to throw the ball and it just plopped down by his sneakers. He was so mad, but when Lady, our cocker spaniel pup grabbed the ball and ran off, he ran laughing after her. I looked at my beautiful wife and we smiled to each other in that way only a man and woman in love with each other can do. The fire whooshed up and the coals got hot. She wandered over to me, a cool can of soda in her hand. She took the soda and placed it on the back of my neck as she wrapped her arms around me. I felt her slight body press against mine and I felt the hardness grow in my pants. She kissed me and around tongue and lips and nibbles the words I love you flowed out like a cool breeze on a hot day. I looked in her eyes and told her I loved her too and the fire was hot, the afternoon hotter and all was well until...

I woke up on my bench, stiff and sweaty, the half bottle of whisky cradled in my hand. My soda had spilled and was covered in scurrying ants so I said screw it and downed the rest of the spirits. I sat up, coughed and spat out a gob. I looked around and saw the sun winking good morning in the east and wondered again where the time went. I was beginning to have trouble telling the coming of night and day, and while this alarmed me, I didn't have time to ponder why. I dug my hand in my pocket and counted my change. One hundred and ninety dollars and some loose coins. So it was true. I really had two hundred dollars to my name yesterday and most of it left today. I sat up, scrubbed my face with my hands and grabbed my guitar case.

On the corner, I opened the case, took my girl out and started in on "Whole Lotta Love". A man with a long snuffly snout in a NYC t-shirt, jeans and round little hipster glasses tapped his paw along with the beat. He pulled out a few bills, sniffed them and dropped them in my case. I moved on to "I Can't Quit You, Baby" and I looked up to see that a huge beetle had creeped up to catch a groove. His antennae waved and his spindly feet snappity-snapped slowly along with the song. He vomited a fifty into the case and scurried along, almost getting run over by an exterminator's truck that ran the the red light. By the time my fingers was bleedin' I was wrapping up "Dazed and Confused". A fat, sweaty walrus in an overcoat flopped by, and flipped a few bills on top of the growing pile. I was about done, but a big 'ol egg sauntered up on skinny chicken legs and requested "I Am The Walrus?" and I said, "No, you are the Eggman, the walrus just left." He cracked up and I scrambled to come up with a song. Finally, I got my beat and played that song that some serial killer stole from the boys from Liverpool. He seemed happy with my song choice and a few bills fluttered down into the case. He turned away, stopped, thought for second and came back. A few more greenbacks dropped into my case. He seemed happy with the song. Or maybe he just got laid. I dunno, but the sun was creeping down the western sky. My case was so full of money that I didn't even bother trying to stuff it in my pockets. I slung the old girl over my back on her strap, closed the case and wondered where I could go with a guitar case full of cash and not get robbed or beaten or both.

I knew there was a cheap little hotel somewhere up the street where I stayed once when I had some extra coin. I thought why the hell not? A bed would be better than the bench and I damn well earned it and could damn well afford it. I headed towards the setting sun.

It didn't take long before I was totally lost. Now, I know my way around this gritty city pretty good, but I have never been in this neighborhood. Fancy apartment buildings lined the street on both sides with well dressed Dobermans and Rottweilers in vests and bowties guarding the lobbies.

I stopped a tall, yellow bird walking the other way and asked him if he knew of a hotel around here. He ruffled his feathers, annoyed at the intrusion, but pointed his wing in the direction I was walking. I thanked him, he clucked something I didn't understand and went on his way. Damn foreigners, they're everywhere these days. Can't chirp a word of Da Engliss. I continued down the street, and foreigner or not, he was right. There was a big ol' fancy hotel on the corner, right by the park. It seemed a bit too fancy, but I walked in anyways and asked the turtle behind the counter how much for a night or two. He told me the price and I set my case down, clicked open the latches and pulled out some greenbacks. He thanked me, sir, and slid a key across the counter with his stubby foot.

I spent the night in white satin sheets and woke up before the sun all dazed and confused. It took me a few to realize where I was. It certainly wasn't my bench cause I didn't have any splinters in my narrow ass. I sat up in bed and took in the room. Nice and big. Soft carpet on the floor, Hoity-toity wallpaper. Mirrors and expensive furniture. I threw the sheets back and went to the big window. The sun was just opening it's big, sleepy eye and I looked a dizzy way down at the street and the big, green park spread out before me. A guy could get used to this. Yesindeedy. But, I was hungry, as usual, and groaned inside at the long walk to Paulette's hot dog cart. I turned from the window and saw a folder on the nightstand with MENU printed in scripty gold letters. I picked it up and looked inside. Hmm. No prices. I sposed everything was free when you was puttin on the ritz. I picked up the tellyfone, dialed a few numbers and told the nice girl on the other end what I wanted to eat. I asked where I had to go to pick it up and she informed me that this was room service. I told her the room didn't need no servicing, I just wanted to get some food. She let me know that my food would be brought up to my room. I thought that was an awful long way for a waitress to walk, but said thanks anyways and hung up. About a little bit later, I was trying to figger out how to turn on the boob-tube when there was a knock on the door. I said c'mon in door's open and a fish in a tuxedo served me breakfast. Bagel with lox and cream cheese. I didn't want to be shellfish, so I rummaged around the case full of money. He said his name was Gill and I tipped him a fin.

After gobbling down my bagel, I sighed contentedly and thought life's been good to me so far today. My belly was full of something besides hot dogs, Gill had flippered the TV on for me and my bare feet were about three feet deep in soft rug. I went in the bathroom and showered up with real soap and shampoo. There was even a razor and some peppermint smelling shave cream. (all free). I lounged the day away in a robe made of the same stuff they make towels outta. It was nice way to kill the day, but, I needed to play, or at least hear, some tunes. I had shit, showered and shaved and realized I only had my grubbies to wear. Caseful of cash or not, I couldn't go ditty boppin' around a fancy place like this smellin' like a felon. I glanced at a curlicue wooden cabinet in the corner and opened the door. Well, well. Full of suits. Real ones, where the pants match the jacket. (free also, cause there weren't no price tags). I grabbed a shiny dark blue one, along with a crisp white shirt and a thin tie the color of a robin's breast. I pulled the clothes on and looked at myself in the mirror. My reflection said not bad. Except for my hair. Long and stringy cause, ya know, hot dogs are more important than haircuts. I looked back in the wooden cabinet that I think they call a war drove, or something like that, makes no sense, but whatever, and saw a hat like The Chairman might wear on the top shelf. I pushed my hair back over my ears and plopped the lid on my head my way, at a jaunty angle, and snapped the brim. Perfect. Except for my bare, stinky feet, which now smelled like a high class hooker; cause of the free soap. I looked at the bottom shelf and there were a buncha shoes lined up like soldiers in a parade. I grabbed a pair of shiny black ones and some socks that felt like ladies underwear and slipped my feet directly into heaven.

Fully spiffy, I grabbed my room key, a few hundred bucks and headed out my room and down the hall. A sharp-dressed penguin in a top hat tapped his brim to me as he walked by and I did the same, back atcha. In the elevator, I saw that I was on the top floor. That explained the dizzy view from the window. I had no idea where the bar was, or if there even was a bar in the place. I looked at the buttons stupidly cause there was a 1 at the bottom, which made sense, but under that was G and a B and an L, which didn't make much sense. Seemed like B for bar was a smart choice, so I reached out to press it. Nothing happened. So I pressed it again. Just then a six-foot tall dormouse in a red vest scurried into the elevator with me. He said,

"Sir, the basement is only for us staff mice. Where would you like to go?

I said "The bar, if you have one", and he told me The Lounge was on the Lobby Level. He pushed the L with his paw and down we went. I made a mental note to remember what the dormouse said.

The elevator doors whooshed open and I stepped out on marble tiles. I glanced around and didn't see a bar, just the front desk where I checked in and some waiting chairs. I wanted a Lounge, not a Lobby. There was a little bitty pretty kitty cat behind the front desk, so I sauntered up and said,

"Hey darlin', where can a thirsty man go around here?"

She pointed her paw down the hall and I gave her a wink and a nod.

I walked down a longish hallway and about halfway, I could hear the grooves. As I got closer, the grooves turned into plump-thumpin bass and drums with a nice topping of horns and strings. Right over the door was a glittery sign that said "The Gold Room". I walked in and was hit with a solid wall of sound. There was an elephant in the room and he was trumpeting out a snappy boogie woogie. A big gorilla, at least five hundred pounds, was ticklin' the skins and ratta-tap-tappin the cymbals. I couldn't help but snap my fingers as I muscled through the crowd and bellied up to the bar.

The bartender nodded to me and I replied

'Whiskey'

He asked, "Makers or...?"

I replied, "I dunno...Jack or Jim?"

He informed that

"Sir, we only serve Glenfiddich or Maker's Mark.
I said "Ok"

He poured me a shot and I downed it straight away. I motioned for another and slapped a Frankie down on the worn oak wood bar. My shot glass was refilled and I told him, he was the

"Best goddamn bartender from Timbuktu to
Portland, Maine. Or Portland, Oregon, for that
matter."
The bartender nodded and said
"Thank you for saying so."

A short, fat bumblebee had buzzed up onto the center stage. He folded his wings and picked up a hollow body Gibson electrical guitar and let us know that the thrill was gone. A cute pup sitting on the next stool informed me that that was B.B. King. I nodded knowingly and tossed her a wink. I soaked in the legendary blues like a hot bath and signaled the best goddamn bartender to fill me up along with the sweet little puppy sittin' next to me. He obliged and I swallowed the liquid fire and tapped and snapped my way through the ditty. The big bee wrapped up with a flourish and took a short bow and sat right back down and the honey flowed from his lips and his fretboard.

A table vacated right in front of the stage, so I nodded to the cute pup to follow me, and she did. We sat at the table and listened to B.B. sing,

"The sound that you're listening to
is from my guitar, that's named Lucille"

When he said if he could sing pop tunes like Frank
Sinatra or Sammy Davis, Jr, he couldn't even do it cause,
"Lucille don't wanna play nothin but the blues"

It made me sad to think his girl only played the blues.

Then he sang,
"I think I'm pretty glad about that, cause don't
nobody sing to me like Lucille"

And I thought about my girl, who only really
sings to me, all alone up there in that fancy room and I
felt the blues land on me like a big ten-ton heavy thing.

After B.B. sang
"One more time Lucille"
five more times, the place erupted in applause. As my little
pup sat up like a good girl and clapped her paws, begging
for more, B.B. buzzed off the stage and landed right in
front of our table. He held Lucille out to me and I put two
fingers in my mouth and whistled as loud as I could for the
bluesman. He shook his head and held the pretty electric
lady out to me. I tapped my chest and he nodded. I shook
my head, and he nodded again. I took the guitar from his
hands and looked at it like an idiot. He bent over, buzzed
something in my ear and took off into the crowd. I don't
know what he told me, but I knew I had a live electrical
guitar in my hand. I looked around, kinda nervous. I

hadn't never played to such a rowdy crowd before. But I took that sweet baby in my hands, knowing full well I was cheatin on my honey and sat down on the stage.

The instrument was warm in my hands. She sat on my lap, her curves fittin just right. She turned her head to me and said,

"You gonna play me, sugar, or just sit there feelin' me up?"

So I did what any man would do with a warm sweety sittin on his lap; I felt her up and down, lookin for that sweet spot. I played her. Soft at first, then harder and then soft again. She moaned and sighed and sang right along with me. I thought about some words and sang,

"I been alone too long
Tryin to sing everybody else's song
But now I know just where I belong"

Lucille seemed to like it cause she sang out pretty along with me. The crowd seemed to like it too, cause they clapped and whistled and hooted. I finished up,

"Street corner been my home
I been all alone
But now I found my own"

And the little pup ran up on stage and licked me right on the lips, the crowd was going wild and the elephant nodded to me and trumpeted out his approval. B.B. buzzed back up on stage and threw a wing around me. I handed Lucille back to him and we both took a bow.

A gentleman doesn't discuss his personal matters in regards to the ladies, but rest assured the pup followed me to my room. The next morning I woke up to dog breath. I gave her a bath and sent her on her way. I'm just happy she didn't give me the fleas. Anyways, after she left, I sat down next to my girl. I picked her up hoping she wasn't too mad at me. She seemed a bit stiff, and gently weeped, when I sat her in my lap, but after a few soft chords, she seemed to loosen up a bit. I pulled out my Master Key and as I softly tuned her up, I explained to her that it's not every day a guy gets to play with Lucille. She wasn't happy about that, which turned out ok, cause she sang the blues in a way that was both sweet and pissy. A good combination.

The crowd seemed to like her attitude and we played the Gold Room every night. We brought the house down Fridays and Saturdays when B.B. buzzed in and did a number with us. I even let B.B. tickle my honey and she liked that. Guess that door swings both ways.

Somehow, my case never runs out of money. I've been here at the hotel now for a few years or ten and I think and everything seems free as a bird now. They gave me a long, shiny car to drive around in, and my suits are always spiffy. I keep my Master Key in my breast pocket and one day, when I was on the way to somewhere important, we rolled up to a corner where some dude was playing guitar. I rolled the electrical window down and listened to him play Dylan. Out of tune. I told the alligator driving the car to pull over for a second. I got out and walked up to the guy. He looked up at me as he belted out,
> *"You better start swimmin'*
> *or you'll sink like a stone.*
> *Oh, the times they are a changing"*

I tapped my foot through the song and when he was done, I tossed a few hundred bucks in his case. The look on his face was well worth it. I turned on my shiny heel back to the car and he started in on "The Joker". I turned back to him, and listened to the song all the way through. When he was done, I reached into my breast pocket, pulled out the Master Key and handed it to him.

AFTERWORD

Call me crazy, but I have this idea that you like to read. (It's not a great deduction on my part, Watson. If you didn't like to read, you wouldn't be here right now.) I like to read too. It's easy: you simply follow the words on the page and, hopefully, it takes you someplace else. If the story is really good, you might even forget you're reading. If it's a novel-length piece, well then you just got a mind movie that lasts longer than a real movie for the amazing low price of whatever the book cost you. Even if you bought it brand new in hardback, you can't beat that kind of entertainment value. Plus, you can read it again and again and even share it with a friend without having to worry about piracy. Writing? Not as much fun as reading. Writing is great if you throw your ideas into some type of word program, or write out longhand (who does that anymore?) or maybe even speak into a recording device or computer gadget of some type. That's the part of writing that makes people like me believe that I love it enough to do it until I draw my last breath. It's exilirating! Thoughts and ideas made real! The problem is that I read my own writing. This results in seemingly endless rewrites and editing and formatting and converting that can literally (pun certainly intended) take years. I suppose if a writer has a publisher with a staff of people who know punctuation and grammar, graphics, file conversions and various and sundry other useful skills, which I don't fluently possess, then this process could conceivably be shortened by days, or even months. If I had a publisher, I'd be like the Lion, The Scarecrow and the Tinman. I will have found my heart, my brain and most of all; my courage to just write and not be bogged down by the technical details. Until then, I will continue to write, no matter how much the back-end pains me. Because, yes, I would love to do this until I draw my last breath.

About the Author

This is my second book. I'm a visual artist, photographer, musician, single dad and sometime writer. I was born in Philadelphia, Pa. and I'm certain my youth in that gritty city shaped the things I make and write about, but I'm not sure I can tell you why. I now reside in the Sunshine State and while it's very nice and serene here with beaches and palm trees, and hurricanes I really love the city with its hustle, bustle, decay, rebirth and unique flavor.

Please take a moment and check out my other book:
The Forbidden Tourist:
An Artist's Journey to Abandoned Places.

Its a pretty specialized book about abandoned insane asylums, hospitals, amusement parks and other weird locations. It might not be for you, but then again, you got this far, so maybe it is. It's illustrated with my original photographs and a chronicle of my time in these places arranged like a travelogue. You can find it on Amazon.com or theforbiddentourist.com

You can also see my original artworks at szabries.com if you're into that sort of thing.

Thank you for reading. I won't say I wouldn't write, paint or create if nobody ever saw my work, but it sure does make it worthwhile.

Thank you for staying with me to
The End.